On the TRAIL of ELDER BROTHER

On the TRAIL of ELDER BROTHER

Glous'gap Stories of the Micmac Indians

Retold by
MICHAEL B. RUNNINGWOLF
(MICMAC NATION)

& PATRICIA CLARK SMITH

Illustrations by
MICHAEL B. RUNNINGWOLF

A KAREN AND MICHAEL BRAZILLER BOOK
PERSEA BOOKS/NEW YORK

Library of Congress Cataloging-in-Publication Data
RunningWolf, Michael B.
On the trail of elder brother: Glous'gap stories of the
Micmac Indians/retold by Michael B. RunningWolf and Patricia
Clark Smith; illustrations by Michael B. RunningWolf.
p. cm.
ISBN 0-89255-248-4 (hc; alk. paper)
1. Gluskap (Legendary character) 2. Micmac Indians.
3. Micmac mythology.
I. Smith, Patricia Clark. II. Title

E98.M6 R86 2000
398.2'089'973—dc21   99-087597

Designed by Leah Lococo. Typeset in Adobe Caslon.
Printed in the United States of America.
First Edition

MICHAEL DEDICATES THIS BOOK
TO HIS SON JOSEPH ISAAC RUNNINGWOLF,
AND TO HIS NIECES BETH AND SHILOH
AND HIS NEPHEW LAWRENCE.

———————————

PAT DEDICATES THIS BOOK
TO HER SONS JOSH AND CALEB, HER NIECE
SHAULA, HER NEPHEW MAX, AND HER
GRAND-GODSON JACKSON.

———————————

TO THE CHILDREN OF THE MICMAC NATION,
AND ALL FUTURE GENERATIONS
OF MICMAC PEOPLE.

ACKNOWLEDGMENTS

THANKS, ABOVE ALL, to the ancestors who shared their stories.

Thanks to our spouses, Kat RunningWolf and John Crawford, who put up with our madness, listened patiently, and gave sage advice.

Thanks to our agent Susan Cohen and our editor Karen Braziller for seeing this book into print. We could not wish for better colleagues.

Thanks to the many people who read or listened to these stories, and who commented and made suggestions: Rita, Jim, Mike, and Denise Clark; James Colbert; Tom Cummings; Gary and Marlys Harrison; David Johnson; Tony Mares and Carolyn Meyer; K.T. Martin; Elsie and Edythe Mocho; Louis Owens; Rich, Janet, Danny, and Chrissy Pascal; Luci Tapahonso; Sophie Wadsworth; Sharon Oard Warner; Jill Williams and Mike Wolfe; Hugh and Barbara Witemeyer.

A special thanks to Victor and Martha Garcia, and to Pat's students in Native American Literature classes at the University of New Mexico.

To all, we say *we'la'lin*.

CONTENTS

Introduction IX

The Coming of Glous'gap 3
Glous'gap and Young Wolf 11
Why the Beavers Are at War with Glous'gap 17
Porcupine and Fisher 21
**How Glous'gap Saved Pine Marten
and Mrs. Bear** 25
Glous'gap and Grandfather Turtle 43
Glous'gap and the Water Monster 57
**How the Sacred Pipe Was Brought
to the Micmac** 65
Glous'gap and Painted Turtle 73
The Boy in the Birchbark Box 81
Glous'gap and Wotjou'san, the Wind Bird 93
Glous'gap and the Little Summer Woman 99
Glous'gap and the Gulls 107
Glous'gap and Wa'sis 117
Glous'gap and the Three Wishes 121
Glous'gap's Farewell 127

Map: Land of the Micmac 132
Micmac Glossary and Pronunciation Guide 133
Further Reading and Viewing 141
About the Authors 144

INTRODUCTION

THE STORIES IN THIS BOOK are told by the Micmac people of the Maritime Provinces, Quebec, and Maine. The Micmac belong to the great body of Algonquin language speakers, and many of these stories are shared among the closely connected Eastern Algonquin peoples known as the Wabanaki, also called the Children of the Dawn, and Keepers of the Sunrise. The Wabanaki are made up of the Micmac, Malicite, Passamaquoddy, Penobscot, and Abenaki tribes and bands. Some of the stories are told even more widely among Algonquin speakers; people as far south as Delaware and as far west as the Great Lakes know of water-hoarding monsters and fearsome lake serpents.

We Micmac were among the first American Indians to have contact and interaction with Europeans coming to these shores, and yet their descendents to this day know little about us. Here we offer a sampling of the many stories that center on Glous'gap, the great being whom we call Elder Brother. Though most of these stories are told among all the Wabanaki, they differ slightly from tribe to tribe. We generally tell the Micmac version.

God is called Gitji Manitou (the Great Spirit) or Nigsgam (Holy Grandfather) or Kesoulk (The Creator), and Glous'gap is the embodiment of his power. It is he who moves about on the earth and who has direct dealings with people and animals. Our stories tell us that Glous'gap cannot live without the people, nor can we live without him. He is our spiritual teacher, the ultimate warrior, medicine-person, and occasional trickster. Some say he is a spirit; others think he is human. In any case, the things Glous'gap says and does are models for the way our people approach life.

The Glous'gap stories embody the laws, morals, and wisdom of the Wabanaki people. Some may think stories like these are of little use today, but they are wrong. Ingenuity, audacity, a sense of humor, cooperation, kindness, the hatred of injustice, the determination to survive—these things always matter. Moreover, the earth is still a place where astonishing things can happen, much as they did in Glous'gap's time among us. These stories unfold in a wonderful world of monsters and magic that is still very recognizably the northeastern woodlands, a world brimming over with intelligent life. Here, whales are irresistibly drawn to come and serve whoever can sing the Micmac whale-summoning song, spring flowers speak to us of new hope, and porcupines are irascible, then as now.

As our title suggests, *On the Trail of Elder Brother* follows Glous'gap through his adventures during the time he lived with our people. When he comes, the earth is still raw and barely formed, and he helps to shape and populate it with creatures and plants. He teaches human beings how to live and how to live together, and he battles on our behalf with the monsters who threaten on all sides. By the time he takes his leave of us, the world has become a more settled place, and the later stories mostly concern the evil that arises from human hearts.

These traditional Micmac stories do not have distinct

beginnings, middles, and ends that leave the characters tidily accounted for. As in all great story cycles, whether Norse or Hindu, Greek or Iroquoian, each tale is one branch growing out of a wide-spreading tree. There are many more Glous'gap stories, and many more parts to each story than we retell here. But you can sometimes see how the story-branches in this book connect and intertwine. For example, certain decisions Glous'gap makes back in the dawn of time infuriate some of the animals, and in years to come the clams, beavers, and moose will continue to take their anger out on him and the Micmac people. Again, Glous'gap's wars with the sorceress Poug'tjin'skwes span many ages, and each meeting of these old enemies is spiced by their past encounters.

Since the seventeenth century, a number of non-Native anthropologists have listened to Micmac storytellers and set down their versions of Glous'gap stories. We list some of these accounts in an appendix. As far as we know, ours is the only book of traditional Micmac stories that have been retold and written down by two Micmac authors. It is also the only account we know of that focuses entirely on Glous'gap's history.

How this book came to be written is a story in itself. At times in our young lives we were being raised within a few miles of one another, but we did not meet until we were middle-aged and living in New Mexico, far from the beaches and woodlands of our childhoods. Michael RunningWolf grew up in Maine and New Brunswick. He is a native speaker of Micmac, a storyteller descended from the very Micmac people who were often interviewed by early anthropologists. Michael learned most of these tales as a child after the chores were done on Friday and Saturday nights, when he and his seven brothers and sisters gathered around the wood stove to listen to his father or his grandmother or some other family member begin a story. In the old way, his grandmother would sometimes bite shapes out of birchbark to illustrate a part of the story. Patricia Clark Smith also grew up in Maine, and she is of Irish, French Canadian, and Micmac descent. Pat is a professor of English at the University of New Mexico, where she teaches Native American literature and creative writing. Together, we have tried to bring the stories of our people to life on the printed page.

We wanted to give our readers the Micmac words for things as often as possible; there is a glossary and pronunciation guide at the back of the book. The map of the north country on page 132 uses Micmac place-names. It traces Glous'gap's trail as he journeys to rescue Pine Marten and Mrs. Bear and marks other sites in New England, the Maritime Provinces, and points beyond where the Glous'gap stories happen. The map and the illustrations were made by Michael, who incorporates into his pen-and-ink drawings traditional designs and symbols from Micmac quill and bead work, hide paintings, and writings on rock and birchbark.

Listen now to the voice of the storyteller, beginning in the old-time way with these words: *Wodin'it atog'agan Glous'gapi* . . . here is a story of Glous'gap!

MICHAEL RUNNINGWOLF

PATRICIA CLARK SMITH

On the TRAIL *of*
ELDER BROTHER

THE COMING
OF GLOUS'GAP

Wodin'it atog'agan Glous'gapi...

S OME SAY THAT GLOUS'GAP was born in
the land of the Wabanaki, but more ancient stories speak of him coming down from Was'ouk, the
Sky World, during the time the world was being

formed by Kesoulk, the Creator. They say Glous'gap made his way across the Sunrise Ocean in a great stone canoe that was really a whole island of granite forested with spruce, pine, and cedar. With him on the island lived some people with the names and natures of different birds and animals—Mrs. Bear and Pine Marten, the Partridge people and the Bluejay folk, Painted Turtle, and the Clam people. The island-canoe finally anchored off the northeast coast, the place the Wabanaki call the Land of the Sunrise. There were no people living on the mainland yet, but it was rumored there were wild people living very far to the west. Just how long ago all these things happened is lost to us now.

Soon after Glous'gap came to these shores, he built a lodge for himself. Right away Kesoulk the Creator gave him work to do. "Take your maplewood bow and dredge out all the rivers and streams of their mud and sludge," Kesoulk ordered. "Make the channels deep and clean so the waters can run smoothly into the ocean." So Glous'gap began clearing all the waterways of the continent, making deep riverbeds that wound their way toward the great salt ocean to the east. He did this by dragging his maplewood bow through the mud and silt, and it was hard, hot work.

By the end of the first day Glous'gap was muddy and exhausted. He trudged along the trail back to his wigwam and sank down on the cool grass before the door of the lodge. After a while he got his second wind and began looking around him, and suddenly he saw something he hadn't noticed before. Coming along the very trail he had just traveled was a lovely young woman, slim and strong.

How had he ever missed seeing her, he wondered? She walked straight over to where Glous'gap was sitting and smiled down at him.

"What are you doing here?" asked Glous'gap.

"I have come to help you," replied the woman in a clear voice. "I am resourceful and young, and I will be good at this work."

Glous'gap had to admit he could use the help, and so he invited her to stay with him in his lodge. The following morning, after the sun had risen from the ocean, Glous'gap and the young woman went out to the waterways and worked very hard all day at cleaning the rivers. They pulled up debris from the beds and dredged silt from the channels so all the waters of all the rivers of the land, mighty rivers and little rivers alike, could make their way smoothly to the sea.

The two returned to Glous'gap's wigwam that evening and were sitting exhausted on the grass before the door when they spied a handsome, well-muscled young man walking toward them along the trail they had just taken home. This time Glous'gap was not so surprised. He suspected this newcomer was part of Kesoulk's plan for his new-forming world. "Come over here!" Glous'gap cried to the young man. "What are you doing here?"

"I've come to help you," the young man replied. "I am young and resourceful, and I'll be good at this work."

"Where have you come from?" Glous'gap asked.

"I have come from Was'ouk, the Sky World," the young man said, and Glous'gap nodded to himself. He invited the young man to stay in his wigwam as well.

The next day all three went forth together to finish dredging out the riverbeds. What with three pairs of strong hands at work, by late afternoon the great task was at last completed. Glous'gap felt satisfied when he saw how beautifully all the rivers now flowed to meet the ocean. Then he raised his eyes from the waters, and he frowned a little. He could see there was more work to be done to make the world the sort of place Kesoulk meant it to be.

Glous'gap turned to the young woman and said, "You know, we have plenty of plants and trees and bushes here, but they have no buds, no blossoms, no leaves, and no fruit. I want you to go around to each growing thing and help it. Give the evergreens fragrant needles, and give them cones as well so they can make more cedars and spruces and pines. Give the oaks acorns, and wrap shining white bark around the birches. Let there be strawberries in the sunny clearings, blackberries in the thickets, and cranberries bobbing in the bogs. Be sure to give each leafy tree the sort of foliage that will turn just the right color in autumn, so we can enjoy scarlet maples and golden beeches and bronze oaks."

The young woman worked hard, and when her tasks were done she proudly showed the splendid trees and plants and shrubs to Glous'gap. He admired them all, but then he rubbed his chin thoughtfully and said, "You know, it would be a good idea to have some birds on these beautiful trees to sing for us."

"I left all my birds back there in the Sky World," the young woman said. "I'd be very glad if we could find some way to bring them here. I really miss them!"

So Glous'gap summoned up all his power and called

upon Kesoulk to send the birds from their home in the Sky World. Down they came, the whole host of birds, wheeling and gliding and flapping and diving through the air, birds of all sizes and colors with their wings gleaming in the sunlight. When they reached the Land of the Sunrise, each bird immediately began to do the very things it was supposed to do. The chickadee flitted in the branches and called out its own name. The loon rocked on the waters of the lakes and laughed. The blue heron waded and fished in the ponds, the red-winged blackbird teetered and trilled from the cattails, the jay screamed, the robin caroled from a bough, and the eagle soared grandly above all, its cries drifting down to Glous'gap and his helpers far below. Glous'gap smiled to hear and see how the birds enlivened the world.

Next, Glous'gap turned to the young man and said, "We need some animals around here!"

Again, Glous'gap summoned up all his strength and called upon the Creator to help him. Now Kesoulk the Creator is the greatest of all beings, but his power sometimes works through Glous'gap, and so it was this time. While his two helpers watched in awe, Glous'gap created the animals, and as he called each to him, he gave it a name. He made the squirrel and called him A'dou'dou'-gwetj, or Chatter. That squirrel was as big as a whale!

"What will you do if I let you loose on the world?" Glous'gap asked A'dou'dou'gwetj.

With that the squirrel leaped over to a towering tree and brought it down with a crash.

"You're too destructive to be so big!" Glous'gap scolded

as he reshaped A'dou'dou'gwetj into the little fellow he remains today.

Then Glous'gap created the first beaver and named him Kwa'bit, or Hard-tooth. Kwa'bit too was as big as a whale. "What will you do if I let you loose in the world?" Glous'gap asked the beaver. Right away Kwa'bit set furiously to work. He gnawed great trees to splinters and built a dam so vast the countryside started to flood from horizon to horizon.

"This won't work," muttered Glous'gap, dismantling the dam. "You'll drown the world we have been working so hard to create if I let you go on being this size." Then he tapped Kwa'bit lightly on the back, and the animal shrank to the size of ordinary beavers today.

Next, Glous'gap tried his hand at creating the moose. He named him Te'am'mous'e, meaning He Strips Things Off Trees, and called him Te'am for short. Te'am was so big that if you were to stand at his feet and look up, you could not see his head. Glous'gap thought to himself, "It's true that a game animal of this size could feed plenty of hungry families, but he's going to trample everything in his path and flatten the forests, the mountains—everything in this beautiful world. It just isn't worth it to make him so big." So Glous'gap tapped the moose lightly on the hindquarters to make him shrink, but Te'am refused to become any smaller. Eventually, Glous'gap was forced to kill that giant moose and start his moose-making over again from scratch, but that is a story for another time.

At last, Glous'gap finished creating all the animals to his satisfaction, and he looked around happily. Everywhere, creatures were burrowing and nibbling, scurrying and skulking, napping and scratching. The mole tunneled blindly in the dank earth, the otter tobogganed down his mudslide and splashed into the river, the bat flittered about at dusk, and the doe stepped quietly through the brush followed by her two dappled fawns. All was as it should be.

Now Glous'gap turned to his two helpers, and he said to them, "My friends, I am going to marry you to one another." The young people looked at each other shyly, and Glous'gap could tell this plan pleased them both. "You will live together," he went on, "and you will have children, and your children will have children. You will dwell all your days in this beautiful world you have helped to make. You can drink its clear water and eat its greens and fruits and nuts. The animals and birds will be your companions here. You will enjoy their grace and their courage, and sometimes they will give up their lives to help feed you and your family. Go now and make a wigwam for yourselves, and begin your lives together."

So the two bade farewell to Glous'gap and walked away hand in hand, looking for a place to build their lodge. Glous'gap watched them go, smiling.

By this story, our people know how our grandparents came down from the Sky World to help Glous'gap, back when the world was new.

GLOUS'GAP
AND YOUNG WOLF

Wodin'it atog'agan Glous'gapi . . .

THE ABENAKI PEOPLE say that Glous'gap formed himself from dust shaken from the Creator's hands. But our Micmac stories tell us that Glous'gap was actually a twin with a younger brother.

Just as much as Glous'gap was good, his brother Utj'bak'tasum, or Young Wolf, was thoroughly evil.

Before they came into this world, the two babies held council with one another in their mother's womb. They talked about the different ways they wanted to be born. Glous'gap said, "I choose to be born in the usual way, just as other babies are." He knew that it would be his job to lead the people, and being born in the way of an ordinary child would help him to be closer to them.

But Young Wolf thought himself too great a being to come forth into the world in such a common manner. He vowed, "When my time arrives, I shall burst out through our mother's armpit!"

As the brothers predicted, so it came to pass. Glous'gap, first-born and eldest, slipped quietly and easily into this world, and his mother smiled to see her beautiful little son. But suddenly she was wracked with terrible pangs quite unlike the normal pains of childbirth. Sure enough, Young Wolf fought and clawed his bloody way out through his mother's armpit, and thus she died in this unnatural birth.

Now both children were sacred, and both were protected against death. The Creator had whispered to Glous'gap that only a blow from a flowering rush could kill him. To Young Wolf he whispered that only a blow from a fernroot would be fatal for him. Each child was told to guard his secret carefully.

The two boys grew up together. One day Young Wolf, who knew their lives were both safeguarded, casually asked Glous'gap just what it would take to kill him. But

Glous'gap, remembering how thoughtlessly Utj'bak'tasum had slain their own mother, thought it unwise to trust his life-secret to this one who seemed to relish death. Still, he said to himself, "It may prove important one day for me to know Young Wolf's own secret." So he said to Young Wolf, "I'll tell you what, my brother, let us exchange secrets. Then each of us shall know the most important thing about his beloved brother."

"All right. You go first," said Young Wolf, and the elder brother agreed.

But Glous'gap was cautious, and he was determined to test Young Wolf. "The only way I can be killed is by the stroke of an owl's feather," he lied. Young Wolf, however, told the truth, saying, "I can be killed only by a blow from a fern-root."

After many days it came to pass that Kwa'bit'tjitj, the son of Great Beaver, tempted Young Wolf to kill Glous'-gap. Now the beavers still hated Glous'gap because of what had happened back when Glous'gap was first creating the animals, when he had forced the giant beaver to shrink to a manageable size. The beavers couldn't help brooding about what mighty dam builders they could have been if Glous'gap hadn't interfered. "I'll do it," said Young Wolf, and taking up his bow he shot Ko'ko'kas the Owl. Armed with one of those big soft feathers, Young Wolf struck his elder brother with it as Glous'gap slept peacefully in the cool green shade of a beech tree. Glous'gap started awake in anger and Young Wolf ran away. But Glous'gap hollered after him, "Ho, Younger Brother! It is not an owl's feather but a pine root that shall be the death of me!"

Some days passed, and peace of a sort seemed to be restored between the brothers. "Let us be friends and go hunting together as we used to," Young Wolf said to Glous'gap, and Glous'gap agreed. They walked a long way into the woods and made their camp beside a pool in a clear, slow-running stream, a place where game animals would surely come to drink in the evening. After setting up camp, Glous'gap felt drowsy from the sun and the walking, and he stretched himself out to take a nap. Once more, Young Wolf came sneaking up on the sleeping form of his elder brother, and this time he smote him on the head with a pine root. Glous'gap came awake with a roar and drove Young Wolf off deep into the woods.

Then Glous'gap sat down beside the stream with his head in his hands. He felt so sad to know that his brother was in no way to be trusted. Glous'gap began picking up smooth stones from the bank and tossing them idly into the water as he thought about his brother and their poor mother, long dead. Now he had lied to Young Wolf twice in order to save his own life. "Of course, the truth is that nothing but a blow from a flowering rush can really kill me," he mused aloud to himself as he tossed another stone into the pool.

Unbeknownst to Glous'gap, all the while he sat there tossing stones Young Beaver was poking about in the reeds nearby, and he had swum over to see what was making the splashing sounds. He immediately sought out Young Wolf to tell him what he'd overheard Glous'gap saying. Young Wolf was so pleased he offered to give Young Beaver whatever present he asked for. The little creature squeezed his eyes shut and cried, "Oh, please, Master Young Wolf, I should so love to have wings like a duck or a goose!" When Young Wolf heard this foolish wish, he just laughed scornfully and told Young Beaver to go back to his pond.

Young Beaver grew very angry Young Wolf's contemptuous treatment of him, and straightaway he went to Glous'gap's camp and confessed what he'd overheard and how he'd carried the secret of Glous'gap's life to Young Wolf. Glous'gap listened carefully to what the small beaver said. He nodded his head, and then he stood up in sorrow. Plucking one of the ferns that grew abundantly in the damp ground by the woodland pool, he set off into the forest searching for Young Wolf. When Glous'gap found his evil younger brother, he smote him so hard with the fern-root that Young Wolf instantly fell down dead. Glous'gap sang the death song over the body of his younger brother and wept bitterly.

The Micmac say the body of Young Wolf lies entombed in the Chic-chouc Mountains, out on the Gaspé Peninsula. He will rise up at the last days of this earth, when Glous'gap will battle all over again the giants and monsters he fought in the olden times, and Young Wolf will lead that terrible army. People will know when that time is coming, for then Glous'gap will shake the ground with a terrible noise. But meanwhile Glous'gap still weeps for the brother he was forced to slaughter in order that the world might be a safe place for beasts and human beings.

WHY THE BEAVERS ARE AT
WAR WITH GLOUS'GAP

Wodin'it atog'agan Glous'gapi . . .

BACK AT THE DAWN of things when Glous'-
gap created all the creatures, the very first
beaver he made was as big as a whale. One day
Kwa'bit, whose name means Hard-tooth, began to

build the home he dreamed of for himself. He wiped out a whole tract of forest just for the wood to make his lodge, and the dam he constructed was so tall the waters began to flood all the country roundabouts. Needless to say, this greatly displeased Glous'gap, who'd worked so hard to dredge out the broad watercourses and make our land beautiful.

"Stop, my friend!" called out Glous'gap the Gitji'ke'-napi, the great man of power. "You'll drown everything we've got here!

Great Beaver, Gitji' Kwa'bit, was too busy to listen. He tried to say, "Go away, Glous'gap," but just then he was swimming off with another stand of huge trees in his mouth, and it came out more like "'O away, 'ous'ap!"

"Come back here!" thundered Glous'gap, and Great Beaver dropped his mouthful of timber and stared defiantly at him.

"I'm building myself a lodge and a dam to suit my needs, and that's all there is to say about that!" he snarled.

Glous'gap said sternly, "Friend Kwa'bit, you are not the only one who has need of a place to suit himself! There are many others whose needs you must consider!"

"No one is as important as I am!" Great Beaver replied. "I am reshaping the world!"

Glous'gap shook his head. "My friend, you're too destructive for your size!" he warned, but Gitji' Kwa'bit paid no attention. He simply eased himself into the water so only his nose, his back, and his broad flat tail were visible. He occupied himself by ferrying stand after stand of trees from the shore to his towering dam.

"I am talking to you!" Glous'gap shouted over the water, but Great Beaver paid no attention.

"'O away, 'ous'ap!" he mumbled again over his shoulder, and to add emphasis to his words he slapped his huge cross-hatched tail down on the water, causing a drenching deluge that sent Glous'gap sailing through the air and dropped him to earth some distance away.

Glous'gap spluttered and stood up, soaked to the bone. He seized an enormous rock and chucked it at Great Beaver. Gitji' Kwa'bit dodged it easily, but when another and then another came flying at him, Beaver began to run. In trying to escape Glous'gap's barrage of boulders, Beaver ran crashing through his own dam, splintering it into many pieces. What a fearful sight! Water gushed everywhere. The flood from that broken dam created the many swamps, bogs, ponds, and lakes that are found in the land of the Wabanaki peoples even to this day.

With all his wild scramble to escape, Gitji' Kwa'bit didn't get very far. When he caught up with Beaver, the dripping Glous'gap howled with laughter as he slapped him on the back, causing him to shrink to his present size. To this day, all beavers feel bitter and vengeful toward Glous'gap when they consider how many forests they might have stripped and what a wonderful world of dammed-up waters they might have made. For that reason, they always choose to make war upon him.

But Glous'gap in his turn has been no friend of the beaver, and in time he slew many of them, and their sleek fur has kept him very warm.

PORCUPINE AND
FISHER

Wodin'it atog'agan Glous'gapi...

L ONG AGO, a great flood covered the countryside. The waters washed away nests and bur-
rows and dens and camps and villages, and all the
creatures were left homeless. Porcupine and Fisher

and Glous'gap, our Elder Brother, the Lord of Creation, all sought refuge on a big uprooted tree floating down the swollen river.

Matta'es the Porcupine did not recognize Glous'gap, and even if he had, it wouldn't have made any difference. Porcupine just wanted to be warm and dry. He dug his claws into the broadest, flattest part of the tree trunk, then raised his quills and forced Glous'gap to take the most precarious perch, among the thin branches straggling in the flood. Every time the current buffeted the tree Glous'gap got dunked in the icy waters. He spluttered and shivered as he clung to the sodden branches.

Pe'gumk the Fisher recognized Glous'gap right away and wanted to help him. He turned to the bristling Porcupine and said, "Please, friend, give up your seat to this fellow. Can't you see he's soaked and chattering with the cold?"

"I don't care!" said Porcupine. "If he doesn't like it, let him swim off and find a tree of his own!"

"Please, friend!" said Fisher gravely, glancing over at the drenched Glous'gap. "Don't talk that way! Can't you see how much this one is suffering?"

"Better him than me!" Porcupine sneered, as the tree careened through even wilder waters.

Fisher tried once again. "O Friend!" he shouted above the roar of the flood, "It is sad that you are acting so selfishly! I've asked you twice now to let this unhappy creature take your safe warm perch. Please, won't you give up your spot to he who is more worthy of it?"

But once again Porcupine refused. "I am the great and mighty Matta'es!" he taunted. "Nothing can move me from my chosen place! If anyone tries to dislodge me, one slap of my tail will be enough to send him howling!" With that, he turned his back to Fisher and raised his quills in fighting form.

Fisher had had enough, and he pounced upon Porcupine. Slashing claws and flashing teeth mixed with flying fur and quills, so that the tree bobbled crazily in the current as they fought. Amid snarls, screams, and yeowls, Fisher at last drove Porcupine off the safe wide trunk down toward the roots half-submerged in the frigid waters. By this time, Fisher could not speak because his mouth was shot full of porcupine quills. But with a gallant wave of his paw, he offered the dry spot to Glous'gap.

Glous'gap saw poor Fisher's injured mouth, and he knew how much it hurt. He sat right down on the broad trunk, drew Fisher near to him, and carefully pulled out all the quills. As the tree rushed ahead on the crest of the great flood, Glous'gap told Fisher, "From now on, Pe'gumk, you will be Porcupine's greatest enemy, and his quills will never again harm you. In this way Matta'es will pay for his arrogance and disrespect."

And so it is, even to this day. Fisher is still the only creature who can fight a porcupine and come away unharmed. When Micmac people come across animal droppings with bits of porcupine quill stuck in them, they know Fisher has passed that way, and they know that once again he has gotten the better of Porcupine, just as Glous'-gap promised long ago.

HOW GLOUS'GAP SAVED PINE
MARTEN AND MRS. BEAR

Wodin'it atog'agan Glous'gapi . . .

1.

IN THE OLD DAYS, Glous'gap lived on an island where he shared a lodge with Pine

Marten, the fellow he liked to call Younger Brother, and Mrs. Bear, the elder he called Grandmother. Mrs. Bear kept the lodge neat and prepared meals and took good care of Glous'gap and Pine Marten.

In those days, a person could be both an animal and a human being at the same time. Sometimes Younger Brother looked like a pine marten, with sleek fur, a pointed snout, and a long bushy tail. But he could also change himself into human shape and be a bright-eyed baby or a lithe young man. It was the same with Mrs. Bear. Sometimes she looked like a shaggy, snuffly she-bear, and sometimes she seemed to be a stout old woman shuffling around the lodge. Even when Pine Martin and Mrs. Bear took on human shape, there was always something about the way they moved and spoke that recalled their animal natures.

Glous'gap and Pine Marten shared many adventures together. Sometimes Glous'gap would lend Pine Marten his magic belt, and then he too could perform wonderful deeds. Pine Marten himself had a special possession. It was a small, ordinary-looking birchbark dish, the kind our people call *witj'kwid lakun'tjitj*. Pine Marten ate all his meals from it. In time of trouble, he could leave the dish anywhere, and Glous'gap would be sure to find it. By studying certain mysterious markings Pine Marten would make on the birchbark, Glous'gap could tell exactly how things were going with his little family.

Now there were many other Indian peoples living on the island with Glous'gap. Each band took on the name and the personality of some particular animal or bird. In those times, the Partridge people had begun to acquire a little power for themselves, and in the way of such things, gaining some power just made them want more. They were very jealous of Glous'gap, the most powerful being of all. So the Partridge people held a council, meeting and drumming as partridges do. They decided that while Glous'gap was off on one of his expeditions, they would kidnap Pine Marten and Mrs. Bear and take them far away. The Partridge people had great hope that Glous'gap would die of sorrow if he were left alone on the island. This only shows how little they knew of Glous'gap's powers!

One crisp November day not long after the Partridge people's meeting, Glous'gap was headed home after six weeks of hunting in the forest. Over his back he had slung a hunting cord strung with the rabbits and ducks he had brought down with his maplewood bow, and he carried a full load of cut-up moose meat as well in a pack he had neatly fashioned from the moose's own carcass. His mouth watered as he thought about the delicious moose-meat stew Mrs. Bear would soon set about cooking for their supper. But when he came to the lodge, Pine Marten and Mrs. Bear were nowhere to be seen. *"Nou'goum'itj!* Grandmother! *Utj'kin!* My Younger Brother!" Glous'gap called out, but no reply came.

Glous'gap spotted the tracks of several people, including those of Pine Martin and Mrs. Bear, leading down to the water's edge. He quickly followed them, and whom should he see at the shore but Win'pe, the most dreaded sorcerer among the Partridge people, setting off in his canoe. With him were his own wife and child, and Pine Marten and Mrs. Bear, whom he had forced to accompany him.

The canoe was still within hailing distance, and so Glous'gap cupped his hands to his mouth and shouted, "Grandmother! Send me back my dogs!" He knew he would need their help if he were to rescue his family. Now Glous'gap's dogs, like Glous'gap himself, could assume any size, and right at that moment they were only the size of squirrels. Mrs. Bear snatched up a *woltes'takun*—a wooden bowl—and set the two dogs afloat in it. It drifted easily to the shore where Glous'gap fished it out of the cold salt water and greeted his loyal pets. The dogs licked his hands and face and quivered with excitement. They thought they would be setting off on a fresh adventure right away to rescue their friends, but they were wrong. Glous'gap just stood and watched as the canoe bearing his family slowly dwindled to a speck in the distance. The dogs whined and looked up at Glous'gap, but he only sighed. At last, when Win'pe's canoe was no longer visible, he turned back to the lodge, the dogs following anxiously behind him.

Meantime, Win'pe was puzzled that Glous'gap did not try to stop him. He thought to himself, "Perhaps Glous'gap is already weakened because of the loss of his dear ones." In any case, he decided to move as quickly as he could. With his family and his prisoners, Win'pe paddled on to Passa'-moog'waddy, at the northeastern tip of what we now call Maine, and from there he ordered the canoe on to Grand Manan. After camping there for a while, he crossed over to Kes'poog'wit, which is where Yarmouth, Nova Scotia is today. And so he went, slowly traveling northward along the coast through Oun'a'mag'ik, or Cape Breton, and at last over to Uk'tuk'kam'kou, now called Newfoundland on maps. If you look at the map of northeastern New England and Canada on page 132, you can trace the trail of Win'pe.

2.

Now whether it was to strengthen his own power or for some other reason, no one knows. But the fact is that Glous'gap remained on his island for seven whole months before he began to pursue his marauding enemy. In high summer, when he felt the time was right, he took his dogs and went down to the beach and stood there looking out to sea, far across the waters. Then in a strong voice he began to sing his whale-summoning song, the song the whales have no choice but to obey.

Soon a small whale breached in the distance and swam gladly along the shore straight to Glous'gap. Glous'gap placed one foot on the whale to test his weight, but the creature was too small and sank under the burden. Glous'gap just thanked him and sent him on his way.

Then Glous'gap sang his whale song again, and this time there came swimming up to him the largest whale in all the briny oceans, a mighty she-whale. Her name was Bootup'skwes. She ferried Glous'gap and his dogs well and easily over the waves to Kes'poog'wit. But Bootup had always been afraid of getting stranded in shallow water, and so she called up to her passenger, "Is land in sight yet?"

Glous'gap, not wanting to get his feet wet, called back, "No!"

And so Bootup went on, slicing cleanly through the

gray waters, with Glous'gap balanced deftly on her back. His hair whipped about him, and the salt spray stung his determined face.

As Bootup swam on, she could begin to make out shells lying on the ocean floor below her, and soon the water grew so shallow that she cried out, "*Moon'as'tabagan'-kwi'tje' an'nook?*" which means, "Isn't the land showing itself as plain as a bowstring?"

But Glous'gap called out to her, "We are still a long way from shore."

They raced on until the water was so shallow that Bootup could hear the song the clams were singing from where they lay hidden under the sand below her. Now the Clam people hate Glous'gap, and this was the song they were singing to her :

> *That one, toss him from your back,*
> *Drown him in salt waters black!*

Luckily, Bootup did not understand the language of clams, and so the song was lost on her. But she knew that Glous'gap could speak the languages of all the creatures, and she called up to him, asking, "What song are those Clam people singing, master?"

"Oh," replied Glous'gap, "it goes something like this," and he sang to her:

> *Koussal koussal koussal koussal*
> *Hurry hurry hurry hurry*
> *Ferry that one, ferry that man,*
> *over the waters swift as you can!*

Bootup obediently plied her tail with all her might, swimming faster and faster—and sudddenly found herself thoroughly beached, high and dry on the shore! She could not believe that Glous'gap would deceive her so badly, and she sang out her whale's lament:

> *Ah, my grandson, nou'tjitj,*
> *Alas, you have been my death,*
> *Now I can never leave the land,*
> *Never again will I swim in the sea.*

But Glous'gap just laughed and sang back to her,

> *Have no fear my grandmother,*
> *Have no fear, nou'goum'i'*
> *Wait and see,*
> *You shall swim in the sea once more!*

Then with one shove of his maplewood bow against her massive forehead, Glous'gap sent Bootup sliding off the beach back into deep water. There the relieved whale splashed and dove, flashing her tail and flukes for joy. But before she headed off she swam up close to shore again and asked Glous'gap shyly, "*K'tin tumakun ak tum'a'we?*"— meaning, "Do you have a pipe and tobacco?"

Glous'gap replied "*A'io*, yes, Bootup, my dear Water Friend. You want tobacco? Well, I have some, and as for me, I am in your debt—so take this!" With that he gave her a short pipe and some tobacco and lit it for her. The great she-whale swam off in high spirits, and Glous'gap smiled, watching the faint cloud of smoke trailing after her.

To this day, if you look out to sea carefully in places where whales pass by, you may well catch a glimpse of Bootup's pipe smoke.

<h2 style="text-align:center">3.</h2>

Now Glous'gap pushed on to the place where Win'pe had camped at O'gum'ke'ge'ok, only to find the site abandoned. But he looked around carefully, and sure enough, there on the ground he found Pine Marten's birchbark dish. He picked it up and studied the secret markings Marten had scratched into the bark. He slipped the dish into his pack and went on following the trail of the evil Win'pe.

Along the way Glous'gap came upon an old man and woman. They knew all about Win'pe capturing Mrs. Bear and Pine Marten, for everyone was gossiping about the way the sorcerer had foiled even the mighty Glous'gap. The old couple told Glous'gap that Win'pe and the others had left a good seven months earlier. They also warned him they had heard rumors that Win'pe had left behind monsters to guard his route so that Glous'gap could not follow him.

Right away Glous'gap suspected that the source of some of these monsters must be Poug'tjin'skwes, that witch for whom our people have many names—Evil Pitcher Woman and Black Cat Woman are two of them. She was just the sort of wicked being Win'pe would be likely to call upon for help. Poug'tjin'skwes had the power to take many shapes and forms. She could appear as one man, or one woman, old or young. She could appear as a bevy of beautiful women, a crowd of tumbling, laughing children, or as a whole army of monsters. Glous'gap would just have to be prepared for every possibility, and he was.

Glous'gap continued to follow the trail of Win'pe. By now it was late August, and the nights were growing colder. On his way, Glous'gap passed a little bog hedged about with rushes and cattails. When he looked closely at the bog, he could see the red of ripening cranberries. "Aha!" said Glous'gap to himself, and he waded into the bog and gathered a good many of the cranberries and stored them in Pine Marten's dish. He had an idea they might come in handy.

At last he came to O'gum'ke'ok, where he found a lodge. There by a fire sat a filthy, ragged, toothless old woman covered with lice. She shook with palsy and seemed near death as she looked up at Glous'gap with clouded eyes and whined, "Please, Grandson, gather me some firewood."

Glous'gap did as she asked. After he brought her the wood, she begged him to help her get rid of the lice. In truth, as Glous'gap could sense, this was no pathetic old woman but Poug'tjin'skwes herself. Furthermore, it was no ordinary lice that swarmed over her but tiny devils full of poisons easily able to kill anyone who came in contact with them.

Glous'gap told the old woman to bend down before him, and one by one he began to pluck the devil-lice from her hair. As he flung each louse down, it changed into a porcupine or a toad. The old woman, of course, bent over as she was, could not see what Glous'gap was doing. Each time he plucked at her hair, she would ask, "Have you found one?"

And every time, Glous'gap would answer, "I have!"

"*Basp!* Crush it!" she cackled each time, and at that, Glous'gap would crush a cranberry. Whenever she heard that little squishing sound, she was sure that Glous'gap was covering his fingers with deadly poisons that would swiftly kill him. As the pile of crushed cranberries grew on the floor of the lodge, so did the numbers of porcupines and toads. Glous'gap herded the creatures carefully under a big wooden bowl. Then he used his powers to make Poug'-tjin'skwes drop off to sleep.

When at last she awoke, Glous'gap was nowhere to be seen, and porcupines and toads were swarming across the floor of the lodge. Poug'tjin'skwes was doubly furious because to her way of thinking, Glous'gap had insulted her. If he had truly feared her as an enemy, he would have slain her as she slept. She roared with anger as she took on her own shape, a toweringly beautiful woman, wild and fearsome. Then she gathered up her devil-friends and made plans to do battle with her enemy Glous'gap another day.

4.

Meanwhile, Glous'gap journeyed on until he came to a narrow pass between two hills. He was very watchful, for he was sure that Win'pe had other surprises in store for him besides Poug'tjin'skwes. Sure enough, there at the pass two savage, giant dogs attacked him, but he set his own two dogs at them. The monster dogs were astonished to see the two tiny creatures who looked like they'd make a mouthful apiece suddenly grow to tremendous size, snarling and baying and slavering.

Glous'gap had an unusual way of training his dogs. When he called them off, yelling "Stop! That's enough!" the dogs knew these words were really the signal to fight harder. So it was this time. "Stop!" shouted Glous'gap, and at that his loyal dogs tore the monster hounds to bits.

Soon Glous'gap came to the top of a high hill covered with golden birches and flaming maples. Summer had already turned to autumn, and Glous'gap was grateful for the northern sunlight that warmed him He stopped in a clearing and gazed across all the land. Afar off he saw a large wigwam, and he sighed, for he could foresee that wicked people lived there, and another battle awaited him. Making his way down the rough slope and ledges, he came to the wigwam and found there an old man and his wife and their lovely daughters. The young women came out and greeted the handsome young M'toulin or medicine-warrior with soft voices and winning smiles.

Now it used to be the custom among our people for a young woman to drape a string of delicious bear-entrail sausages around the neck of a young man she admired, and sure enough, the daughters came toward Glous'gap bearing strings of sausages. But these particular sausages were enchanted, and if one of those women had succeeded in draping a string of them around Glous'gap's neck, it might well have been the end of him.

The young women were unaware that Glous'gap

brought a new kind of magic into our world, and did not realize he could see into their bad hearts. They thought they had tricked him completely, and they danced up to him smiling and swaying their slender bodies invitingly as they waved the enchanted sausages in his direction. Glous'-gap gaped and grinned foolishly, acting for all the world like a young man who wanted very much to be courted. As the women danced ever closer, Glous'gap's dogs, who can always smell magic afoot, began to growl.

"*Kous!*" Glous'gap shouted, which means "Stop!" Of course, the dogs recognized that word as their signal to attack, and they sprang upon the young women. With a flash like a brush fire exploding into life, the witches burst into their own dreadful forms, not lovely young women at all but she-fiends with bloodied lips, burning eyes, and foul breath. A battle followed, the likes of which had never been seen before in the land of the Dawn people. The ground trembled, huge boulders splintered, and water sloshed out of the lakes. All the while, Glous'gap kept calling gleefully to his dogs, "Stop, you hounds! Can't you see these are my dear sisters? Come away, you bad dogs!" The dogs fought fiercely until the witches ran off, shrieking and cursing and sobbing.

Glous'gap then strode across the clearing and lifted the flap of the wigwam. There sat the old sorcerer and his wife, fully expecting to eat Glous'gap for their supper. They stared at him in disbelief as he asked with mock politeness, "Are you hungry? Would you two care for some sausages? Well then, here they are, and may you savor them!" With that, he looped the strings of enchanted sausages about their necks, instantly rendering them powerless. Then he slew them with one blow, called his dogs to his side, and went on his way.

5.

After hard journeying Glous'gap reached the Strait of Kamsok just as the first snows were beginning to fall. Again he sang the whale-summoning song, and a whale arose from the depths of the winter ocean to ferry him across the water. Glous'gap circled around Oun'a'mag'ik, coming upon many old camps Win'pe and his captives had left behind. The fires of the camps were drifted over with snow, the ashes long cold. At one such place, Pine Marten had planted another birchbark dish for Glous'gap to find. From the secret marks upon it, Glous'gap learned how long his beloved ones had been gone from that camp and how much they were suffering as the slaves of Win'pe, and he set his heart even more firmly upon finding them. He followed their trail to Uk'tu'tun, which people call Cape North, and there he found that the enemy party had set off only three days earlier for Uk'tuk'kam'kou, the great island of Newfoundland. It was the very heart of winter now, but at least the trail was growing warmer. Once again Glous'-gap sang his irresistible song, and once again a willing whale appeared to carry him across the sea.

Once he landed, he had scarcely traveled a mile inland before he knew he was nearing what he sought, for he found the still-smoking embers of a fire. Swiftly he followed the trail until he came upon Win'pe's encampment. Then Glous'gap hid himself beneath the snow-laden branches of a giant blue spruce and studied the situation. Pretty soon Pine Marten came out of the lodge and began poking sadly around in the deep snow for firewood. Glous'gap could see that Younger Brother was terribly thin and shivering in his scanty but well-mended clothes. Glous'gap knew right away who had kept those clothes mended. It was Mrs. Bear, of course, trying to her best to help Pine Marten survive captivity.

Marten was so deep in despair he did not even hear Glous'gap softly signaling him. Finally, Glous'gap tossed a small stick at Pine Marten's feet, and the young fellow looked up in surprise. At first he thought it was just a twig that had fallen from a tree, but then he caught sight of Glous'gap. Marten started to cry out "Elder Brother!" but Glous'gap fiercely motioned him to be silent.

"Wait until it grows dark, " he said, "and then I'll come into the lodge. For now, just go tell Nou'goum'i, my grand-mother, that I'm here."

Sure enough, late that night Glous'gap stole toward Win'pe's very lodge. A fresh fall of snow muffled his approaching footsteps. Inside the lodge, the evil sorcerer was snoring in the warmest spot near the embers of the fire. Mrs. Bear, hearing a tiny rustle of movement at her back, turned over and beheld Glous'gap by the light of the dying fire. She was so overjoyed to see him that she faint-ed, and Glous'gap knelt beside her and cradled her shaggy head in his lap until she recovered. Mrs. Bear whispered very quietly to Glous'gap about how hard Win'pe made her and Pine Marten work and what poor rations he fed them.

"Never mind, Grandmother," Glous'gap whispered back. "Endure him for just one night longer, Nou'goum'i, and we'll soon have our revenge on Win'pe."

Then he hastily gave some instructions to Pine Marten and bade them both to say nothing of his visit. By then the snow had let up, and a half-moon was shining. Glous'gap melted once again into the shadows between the snow-laden spruces and pines.

Now every morning of his captivity Pine Marten's first job was to fetch the water for the whole camp while he tended Win'pe's stinking, squalling devil-baby in its a'ti-gan'igan, or cradleboard. Glous'gap had told Marten that on this day he must bring Win'pe the filthiest water he could find. So when Win'pe kicked Marten awake at daybreak, Marten did not go as he usually did to fill the buckets with new-fallen snow and bring them inside the lodge to melt into clean fresh water. Instead he shouldered the cradleboard and went straight to a nearby swamp. There he broke the thick ice and dipped up buckets from the oozy, muddy bottom. Then he crumbled old rabbit and deer droppings into the thick, smelly water, and for good measure he threw in the matted hair of a dead skunk he had found. Ever so meekly, Pine Marten offered this foul concoction to his master.

Win'pe sniffed at the reeking cup suspiciously and then poured it out on the ground, swearing a blue streak. "*Uk-se!*" he spat, tossing the bucket angrily at Pine Marten. "Go and bring me clean water!"

Instead, Pine Martin defied the furious sorcerer. He shrugged off the cradleboard and threw it, baby and all, down in the ashes next to the fire. Win'pe's wife screamed and snatched up her bawling devil-child. Then Pine Martin ran pell-mell out of the lodge toward the snowy thicket where Glous'gap lay in hiding, calling out, "Elder Brother! Elder Brother!"

Win'pe was right behind him. His eyes gleamed red with anger, and the veins at his temples bulged. "Go ahead and call upon your precious brother! " he screamed. "He can't help you now! He's far to the south, mooning away on the island where we left him! Cry out as loud as you want, for it's your turn to die, you miserable little weasel!"

Glous'gap's scheme worked. Pine Marten so aroused Win'pe's wrath that he lost the perfect calm control a sorcerer needs to command his evil forces. Win'pe's magic was overcome by his own rage.

Now Glous'gap stepped out of hiding and stood before Win'pe in all his shining power. The sorcerer, sizing up the situation, drew back a few paces to try to gain possession of himself once again. With great calm and steady will, Glous'gap raised every drop of power within himself. As the magic stirred, Glous'gap grew and grew until he towered far above the tallest pine, and the pines in those days were far taller than the ones we know. The Lord of Men and Beasts laughed with delight as he shot upward until he was far above the clouds, and he seemed to be heading straight for the very sun. Far below, Win'pe cowered, tiny as an ant at Glous'gap's mighty feet.

Glous'gap held this quivering sorcerer of the Partridge people in great contempt because he'd acted so underhandedly and treated decent people so badly, and thus he scorned to fight any real warriors' contest against him. Instead, Glous'gap reached down and tapped the sorcerer lightly with the tip of his maplewood bow, as if Win'pe were a dog that needed to be disciplined. At once, Win'pe fell dead. "And that's that," said Glous'gap.

Glous'gap returned to his normal size. He looked around for Win'pe's wife and baby, but they had vanished, no doubt gone to join some of their evil relatives. Then Glous'gap called Mrs. Bear and Pine Marten and his two loyal dogs to come out of hiding. They went about gathering up food and blankets, and then the little party shouldered their packs. With Glous'gap's dogs racing joyfully ahead, the three of them set out through the snow, heading south on the long journey back to their island.

GLOUS'GAP AND
GRANDFATHER TURTLE

Wodin'it atog'agan Glous'gapi . . .

AFTER THE FINAL SHOWDOWN on New-foundland with Win'pe, the evil sorcerer of the Partridge people, Glous'gap paddled his canoe all the way over the icy waters to Pictoug, or, as the

English and French say, Pictou. The name of that place means "bubbling" in Micmac, and it is so named because a whirlpool churns nearby and the waters there are always frothy. In those days there was a winter encampment of more than a hundred wigwams at Pictou, and in that village dwelt an older man whom Glous'gap truly loved. He was called Mik'tjitj, or Turtle.

Now Turtle was not a great man by any means. He wasn't very good-looking, and he had few possessions. People didn't consider Turtle clever or witty or wise. He seemed to have no talent or skill that would cause him to stand out. The others in the village thought him poor, lazy, and past his prime. But out of all others, Glous'gap chose Turtle to be his adopted *nigsgam'itj,* or grandfather. The truth is that Turtle was a wonderful storyteller, though no one but Glous'gap ever bothered to listen to him. Moreover, he had a kind heart, and he bore all the hardships of life so good-naturedly that Glous'gap couldn't help loving him. He resolved to help Turtle rise in the world.

Glous'gap himself, of course, was a handsome man who carried himself proudly. Indeed, he was especially admired by all the women, old and young alike. When he arrived at Pictou, every family wanted him to be a guest at their lodge, but Glous'gap begged off so he could stay with Mik'tjitj, his beloved Grandfather Turtle. Turtle knew all the old-time lore, and his stories delighted Glous'gap. He truly loved this elder.

Now as is usual at Micmac winter encampments, a great feast and celebration were planned. During the warm months, the people usually traveled in small parties to hunt, fish, and gather plant food. Winter was the time when they drew together in larger numbers around the fires and shared many things. They would sing the Gathering Song together and make their Winter Count. They would recite to one another the names of all who had been born and all who had died in their families since the last snows had fallen. If someone had brought down an unusually large moose, or if there had been a big meteor shower, or bright flarings-up of the Northern Lights, they noted that. If there had been an especially good or poor run of eels or salmon at a certain place, that was told as well. Winter Count helped the people keep in touch with each other and record what was going on in the world around them year after year.

Many other doings happened at these wintertime comings-together, including lots of games and competitions. There were snowball fights, snowshoe races, wrestling matches, and a game called snow-snake, in which the players saw who could slide a staff painted like a snake the farthest distance along an icy trough. Then there was *bag'a-tou'we*, a very rough-and-tumble game like field hockey that was not for the faint of heart, as you shall hear later.

Glous'gap himself didn't care to do any of these things, but he said to Turtle, "Grandfather, aren't you going to take part in some of these games? All the young women will be there watching, you know, and I've been thinking that you shouldn't have to live all by yourself. Haven't you ever thought about getting married?"

Grandfather Turtle shook his head and smiled ruefully. "Oh, no," he replied. "I'm afraid I'm too poor, too old, and just too plain. I think it's better if I just sit here alone in my lodge and smoke my pipe and think over the stories from the old times. What do I have to offer any woman? I don't even have any clothes that are fine enough for feast-going."

"Clothes!" Glous'gap exclaimed. "Is that really all that's stopping you from joining the fun? Why, I can stitch up a fine mantle and leggings for you in no time, and they won't ever wear out, either. I tell you, Grandfather, all it will take to make a new man of you is some new clothes!"

"Is that so, Grandson?" mused Grandfather Turtle. He looked thoughtful. "Can you make over the insides of a person as well?" he asked shyly.

"By the Great Beaver!" Glous'gap avowed. "That's a harder job, but it can be done! If I weren't so busy setting things right in this world, I'd do it this minute. But I promise you this, Grandfather. Before I leave this village I'll bring about the transformation you're wondering about. For now, though, let's start with your new clothes. And as for taking part in the games, all you have to do is borrow my magic belt, and you'll do well."

Once Turtle tied on Glous'gap's belt, he appeared many years younger than his true age. Then Glous'gap dressed Turtle in the mantle and leggings he made for him out of soft deerhide. The clothes were most becoming, and suddenly Turtle seemed not only young but good-looking as well. Glous'gap promised him, "From now on, Grand-father Turtle, when you walk in human form you will be the handsomest of all men. When you walk as an animal, you will be one of the hardest creatures to kill on the face of the earth because of your patience and toughness." With

Glous'gap's words of promise in his heart, Turtle set out to join in the feasting and the games.

Now the *sagama* or chief of the Pictou had three daughters. All were lovely, but the youngest was thought to be the most beautiful woman in all the Land of the Sunrise. All the young men of Pictou desired her, and they vowed to kill anyone who won her hand. Because he usually kept to himself, Turtle had never seen this young woman, but that was about to change.

Turtle took part in several games, and just as Glous'gap promised he made a good showing at snow-snake and snowball throwing. Afterwards, the people staged a give-away ceremony in the center of the village. Turtle stopped to watch as families brought out armloads of different goods and set them down for others to choose from. There were fur robes and berrying baskets, quillwork boxes and clam-shell necklaces, fishing-spears and bowls of dried meat and corn. The chief's youngest daughter came out of her father's wigwam carrying a nicely tanned moosehide to contribute to the giveaway. She was slender and lithe, and she smiled sideways at the handsome, young-looking Turtle as she walked past him to place the moosehide on the ground with the other goods. Turtle could not take his eyes off her. All through the night while the feasting, drumming, and singing went on and on, Turtle kept stealing glances at her.

Late that night Turtle returned to his lodge, where he handed Glous'gap back his magic belt. With that, all his youthful appearance fell away, and he looked his true age once again. But as Glous'gap had promised, Turtle remained handsome, in the way of a very dignified elder. He and Glous'gap sat and shared a pipe beside the low glow of their fire. Then Turtle revealed his heart to Glous'-gap. "I've seen the one I want for my wife," he sighed, "but I have no hope of winning her."

"Have courage, Grandfather," Glous'gap said. "Don't you remember that I promised to bring about a transformation in your life?"

The very next day Glous'gap went as an envoy to plead Turtle's cause. He took a lot of *oul'nap'skouk*, or wampum, to the chief's lodge, where he proposed Turtle as a husband for the youngest daughter. The young woman's mother was quick to agree. That was a little surprising, because Turtle had no great reputation. Moreover, it was most unusual for a young woman to be married before her older sisters were wed. But this mother was wise, and she trusted Glous'gap when he vowed that Turtle would make her youngest daughter the best of husbands. She accepted the wampum as her daughter's bride-price.

The chief's daughter built a birchbark-covered wigwam and made up a marriage-bed of pine and spruce boughs covered with a thick white bearskin. She was not at all reluctant to marry the handsome young man she had noticed at the games, the one who kept casting glances at her during the giveaway that followed. But when it came time for the marriage to be celebrated, there stood Turtle, beaming with pride and happiness to be sure, yet now looking his true age. The young bride was dismayed, but all the arrangements had already been made, and so the two were married. That evening, husband and wife and

Glous'gap were feasted at her family's lodge with a wedding supper of dried berries, deer meat, and corn soup. Then Turtle led his bride to their own lodge to begin their life together.

Weeks passed, and the winter wore on. By and by, Turtle's wife began to think that her new husband was rather lazy. Instead of going off on hunting parties with the other men, he preferred to spend the cold and snowy days sitting by the fire and telling stories. She thought the stories were pleasant to listen to, but meantime their larder was getting very low.

Finally, the young woman placed her hands on her hips and scolded, "Just look around you, Turtle! There's not so much as a scrap of meat in this lodge! If you don't bestir yourself and go out hunting as a man is supposed to do, we'll both soon starve!"

"Oh, all right, my dearest," said Turtle good-naturedly, and he strapped on his snowshoes, took up his bow and arrow, and stepped outside into the snow. His wife slipped out of their wigwam after him to make certain he was really going hunting as he said. Sure enough, there went Turtle, setting off for the woods at a brisk pace.

Now it takes most people a while to find their balance on snowshoes, and Turtle was way out of practice. The poor old fellow hadn't gone very far before he tripped over his own snowshoes and landed FLUMP! in a snowbank. His wife looked on with disgust to see Turtle spluttering on his back with his arms and legs waving wildly in the air. She ran straight back to her family's lodge and told her mother, "That Turtle you made me marry is absolutely worthless!

Why, he can't even snowshoe straight!" She wept bitterly to think of all the fine, capable Pictou boys she might have wed.

But her mother smiled, and went on with her sewing. "Don't worry," she told her daughter. "He will turn out to be a good husband yet. You just have to be patient."

A few days later Glous'gap said to Turtle, "Tomorrow there will be a great game of *bag'a'tou'we*, and you must join in. But because you've made enemies of all the young men here at Pictou by marrying the chief's youngest daughter, they're going to try to kill you during the game. They'll all pile on you and try to knock you down and trample you to death, and then they can claim it was just an accident. Now, this attack is going to happen when the play has reached a spot very near your father-in-law's place. So you may escape them, I'm going to give you the power to jump high over that lodge. You'll be able to do this twice with no trouble. The third time, though, won't be easy, and I'm sorry about it, but that's just the way it is."

All came to pass just as Glous'gap predicted. The young men of Pictou did indeed try to kill Turtle. The game was hard-fought, and the players swatted and smashed at each other with their sticks, vying for control of the squirrel-gut ball. Bruising blows landed on arms, legs, and faces. The players were all battered and bloody as they came running through the village. When they finally reached the lodge of the chief, they began to crowd in on Turtle. To escape them, Turtle jumped, and the jump turned into a soaring leap that took him sailing high above the wigwam. He landed safely in the soft snow on the other side, just as Glous'gap said he would. Twice he did this as the angry men tried to crush him by their weight and number, but the third time he got caught in the lodge poles. There hung poor Turtle, dangling in the smoke rising from the fire below.

Glous'gap was seated inside the lodge, visiting with the chief. He heard a commotion above and looked up through the smokehole to see Turtle suspended there. "Grandfather!" Glous'gap called up to him. "I will now make you into the Great Chief of the turtles! You shall have many descendents after you!"

Turtle had no choice. He just hung there, and Glous'gap smoked him for a good long time. He smoked him over that fire for so long that his skin toughened into a hard shell, and the marks of that smoking can still be seen on turtles' shells to this day. Glous'gap then removed all Turtle's intestines except for one short length of gut. Then he destroyed the rest.

Turtle cried out in pain and fear, "Grandson, you're killing me!"

But Glous'gap replied, "No, Grandfather! I'm giving you a long life! Now you will be able to pass through the fire and no feel pain. You will be able to live on land or in water, wherever you choose."

Mik'tjitj the Turtle still felt scorched and sore, but he gave thanks at Glous'gap's words. All this power was coming to him just in time, for soon he would have need of it.

The very next day, right before all the young men of Pictou were setting off on a hunt, Glous'gap said to them, "There is one among you who will come out far ahead in this day's hunt." The young men all smiled, each one certain he would prove to be the best hunter, and then they headed into the forest. Only Turtle lingered behind.

"Soon those men will seek once more to take your life," Glous'gap warned him. Upon hearing this, Turtle nodded. He jumped up and soared into another magical flight, passing high over the heads of the hunting party. He alighted deep in the forest, far ahead of the others. There he brought down a fine big moose, and he dragged it over beside the trail he knew the other men would be following on snowshoes. When the hunting party came upon him, there he sat, leaning back against the moose carcass, smoking his pipe and waving cheerily to them. By this time they were cold and exhausted from their long trek. They beheld Turtle sitting there with his moose, smoking his pipe and looking so well-rested, and then they thought about the beautiful wife he had awaiting him at home, and it all drove them wild with envy. Together, they plotted once again to kill him.

Glous'gap had come along with the hunters, and now he was getting ready to head back to Pictou. He could read people's hearts and minds, so he took Turtle aside and warned him, "These men will build a bonfire and throw you into it, thinking to roast you. Grandfather, go along with what happens, and I promise you will feel no pain. When the roasting doesn't work, next they'll threaten to drown you. Beg and plead with them not to do it. Implore and beseech them not to throw you in the water until they come to think that drowning is the one sure method of murdering you." Then Glous'gap said goodbye to Turtle and set off back toward Pictou.

Again, all happened just as Glous'gap had foretold. Glous'gap had no sooner gotten out of sight than the young men built a raging fire and tossed Turtle into it.

Tired after his long exciting day, Turtle simply rolled over and went to sleep there at the heart of the flames. When the fire burned down and at last he awoke, the astonished young men heard him call out, "Bring more wood! It's a mighty cold night, and I have no desire to freeze to death!"

Then those men snatched Turtle out of the spent fire and began to argue among themselves about what they should do with him. "Let's drown him," said one fellow.

Hearing this, Turtle began to whimper and plead with them, "Please, my brothers! Don't drown me! Oh, oh, anything but that! Chop me into bits, or toss me off a high cliff, as you wish, but please don't drown me in the sea!" Of course, they resolved to do just that, and they dragged him kicking and screaming toward the shore. Turtle fought bravely, tearing up trees and clawing at rocks, but it was no use. The young men overpowered him and forced him into a canoe. They paddled a long way from shore and threw him overboard, and they laughed as they watched him sink from sight, far in the cold gray depths of the ocean. Certain now that Turtle was dead, they canoed back to shore, rejoicing.

The next day brought a sudden thaw, and the young men remained camped on the shoreline, not wanting to slog their way back to Pictou through all the slush and melting snow. Around noon, one of them spotted something like a dot on a rock about a mile offshore. "What kind of creature can that be?" the young men asked themselves, and two of them volunteered to take a canoe out and investigate. The rock rose about a foot above the waterline, and as they drew close to it, they could see that dot was none other than Mik'tjitj, Grandfather Turtle, by no means drowned but sunning himself and enjoying the pleasant break in the weather. When he saw them paddling up to his rock he was sure they were coming to recapture him, and thus without so much as a farewell Turtle slipped off his basking place into the cold salt water and swam away. In memory of the captivity and the abuse Mik'tjitj endured, all turtles slip themselves into the water in just that way whenever they see someone coming.

Turtle swam back to Pictou and lived happily with his wife. By shooting that moose he had proven to her that he could provide well for her and still have plenty of time for telling stories, and from that time on all was harmonious in their lodge. The young men never dared to bother him again, since it was plain to them that Turtle possessed some important magic. In the autumn Turtle's wife bore him a son, and life seemed very good.

The following spring, Glous'gap dropped by to visit Mik'tjitj and his family. He had been busy as usual setting the world to rights, but now he wanted to see his grandfather and his wife and their baby. While Glous'gap and Turtle were sharing a pipe, the child suddenly began to cry. "Oh-wah! Oh-wah!" the little one shrieked. His mother was off gathering wood, and Turtle was at a loss as to how to comfort his little son.

"Don't you know what your own child is saying?" Glous'gap asked Turtle sternly.

"Indeed I don't, Grandson," said Turtle with all the bewilderment of a new father, "unless perhaps he is speaking the language of the spirits of the air, the *mous'i'gisk*, which no one else knows."

"Humph," retorted Glous'gap, feigning great surprise at Turtle's bafflement. "It's plain enough to me that he wants eggs, for he's saying 'Oh-wah! Oh-wah!' and I imagine that's the same as 'oh'wahn, oh-wahn.' Surely you haven't forgotten that's the word for egg in our language?"

Still holding the screaming child, Turtle's face furrowed with concern. "But Glous'gap, I don't have the least idea where to find any eggs," he said.

"Well, try digging in the sand right around here, Grandfather. Maybe some will turn up," Glous'gap told him.

So Turtle laid his little son down carefully on a bearskin robe and begin to dig in the warm sand around his lodge. To his astonishment, he found many eggs of all sorts, and he turned them over in his hands and marveled at them. He looked up at Glous'gap, but Glous'gap just grinned and winked at him. Then Turtle boiled one of the eggs until the insides were soft and runny, and he fed it to his little son. Sure enough, it quieted the little one, and the child's mother soon got home, much to Turtle's relief.

Ever since that day, turtles lay eggs in the sand to keep their own race going, and Turtle's descendents still honor Glous'gap for all the magic he worked on their ancestor's behalf.

GLOUS'GAP AND THE
WATER MONSTER

Wodin'it atog'agan Glous'gapi...

I N THE EARLY DAYS when Glous'gap created
the very first Micmac village, he taught the people everything they needed to know in order to live
well. From him they learned how to stalk deer and

how to catch salmon, how to build fires and set up wigwams and sew clothing from buckskin. Glous'gap showed them which plants were good to eat, and pointed out which ones were poisonous, and others which could be made into medicines to heal their bodies and spirits. He taught them the names of all the stars. He taught them songs of great power and showed them how they might speak well when they met together in council. He taught them the art of war and the art of keeping peace. From him they learned the proper way to make their prayers to the Creator and how to be kind to one another. The people had all the knowledge they needed, and they dwelt together happily. All was going well, just as Glous'gap intended.

Now this first Micmac village was built beside a stream. It always flowed abundantly with pure icy water, and the people were grateful for it. But one day it suddenly ran dry. There was nothing but a little slimy ooze to be found in the streambed. "Perhaps the water will flow again when the autumn rains return," the elders said, but when autumn arrived the streambed only became choked with drifted leaves. In the springtime when the snows melted and most brooks ran swiftly, that stream remained a sluggish trickle.

"What shall we do?" the people asked themselves. At last the elders counciled and decided to send a young man northward toward the source of the spring to discover what he could.

The man they chose walked along beside the streambed for a long time. It was a dreary journey, for all the leaves were sere and rattled in the breeze. Dead fish lay rotting on the dry banks of the stream. No birdsong brightened his steps and no squirrels scolded him from the branches, for all the creatures had abandoned their old homes and gone in search of water. He felt very lonely walking along those desolate banks.

At last the man came to a village where he was surprised to see that the people were not like human beings, for they had webbed hands and feet. They did not have hearts like real human beings, either, for they were selfish and unfriendly and did nothing to welcome the stranger into their midst. The man looked around him and noticed that in the village of the webbed-footed ones the stream widened out just a little, though the water was still brackish and stinking. The man was very thirsty after his journey and asked to be given just a half-cup of that foul water.

"No, we can't give you even a single drop unless our great chief gives us permisssion," the webbed-footed ones replied. "He is a very great chief indeed, and all the water is for him alone."

"Just where is this great chief of yours?" the man asked.

"Follow the stream further north, further north, further north" said the people of the webbed hands and feet, "and you'll be sure to come upon him."

The man did as he was told and walked along until he spied something looming ahead of him. Then he shook with terror as he saw the great chief of whom the webbed ones had spoken. This creature was as big as a mountain, with a grinning mouth that stretched a mile from ear to ear. His yellow eyes stared out of his head like two enormous pine knots. His swollen body was covered with ugly warts. This creature had made himself a huge burrow at the source of the stream and dammed it all up to create a great reservoir. Now almost no water made its way to the streambed. He had also fouled the reservoir and made it so poisonous that fetid mists hung above its oily surface. The monster glared at the man and roared, "Little fellow, why are you here?"

The man gathered up his courage and said, "I come from downstream, where our only brook has run dry because you are hoarding all the water. We need you to give us some, and please, while you're at it, would you also stop making it so thick and muddy?"

The creature only blinked and said with a deep rumbling voice:

> 'I don't care!
> I don't care!
> I don't care!
> For water,
> for water ,
> for water,
> go elsewhere!

The man said, "We really need the water. Our children and all the animals and plants are dying of thirst."

But the monster only replied,

> Go away!
> Go away!
> Go away!
> Just begone

begone
begone
or I'll swallow
swallow
swallow
you today!

And with that the monster opened his cavernous mouth wide. Inside his maw the man could see the many things the monster had already swallowed, bears and pine trees and moose, even whole villages! Then the monster blinked at the man a few times, opened his mouth, and flicked out his pale, sticky tongue. At this the poor man lost every last shred of courage, and he turned and fled.

Back at home he told the people, "We are lost! This creature wants all the water for himself, and if we try to fight, he'll swallow us whole, village and all."

"What shall we do?" they cried. "We cannot live without water!"

Even from afar, Glous'gap could see the grieving village of drought-ridden people. He said to himself, "I must make that stream flow again, so the people can have water."

Glous'gap prepared himself for battle. He covered his body with paint red as fresh heart's blood. He hung two huge clamshells from his earlobes for earrings. He stuck a hundred black eagle feathers on one side of his scalplock and a hundred white eagle feathers on the other. He painted bright yellow rings around his eyes, and then he made himself twelve feet tall and screwed up his face into a fierce mask of anger. He stomped the ground and let out his mighty war-cry, and earthquakes shook the Land of the Sunrise. Then he snapped off a huge mountain with his hand, and from that mountain he chipped himself off a giant flint knife sharp as a weasel's tooth. Now at last he was ready. Lightning played about him and eagles circled above him as he strode upstream.

"I want water!" Glous'gap told the webbed-footed people when he appeared in their village. He so frightened them by his sudden presence that they brought him a little bit of muddy water. "I'll get more and better water!" Glous'gap said as he dashed the ladle of stale water away from himself in distaste. And so he continued upstream, where he confronted the monster.

The creature eyed Glous'gap and grumbled, "Little man, what do you want?"

Glous'gap hollered back,"I want good water and plenty of it for my people!" At this, the creature only laughed:

> *Ho-ho! Ho-ho!*
> *All the waters are mine!*
> *All the waters are mine!*
> *Go away! Go away!*
> *Or I'll kill you today!*

"Slimy lump of mud!" shouted Glous'gap, and he fell upon his enemy, and they fought in a battle that shook the very mountains to their roots and set swamps afire with lurid light.

The creature opened his huge maw to gulp down Glous'gap, but Glous'gap made himself far taller than the tallest pine, so even that gaping monster-mouth could not contain him. Then Glous'gap drew from his belt his great flint knife, and in one swift motion he slit the monster's belly open. A torrent of foaming water gushed from the wound and carved a new path through the dry land. Glous'gap smiled to see the deep clear river rushing past the village of the people of the webbed hands and feet, past the village of the Micmac, and onward to the great Sunrise Ocean. Nevermore need anyone go thirsty.

Once the waters were set free Glous'gap grasped the monster in his mighty hand, and he squeezed, and squeezed, and squeezed. He squeezed the belly-wound shut so it mended, and he kept on squeezing until the monster became very small, little more than the size of a person's fist. Then he flung the creature into a nearby swamp where it leapt off into the cattails, still croaking "Go away! Go away!" The greedy water-monster got squeezed right down into a bullfrog, and even now Bullfrog's skin is wrinkled because Glous'gap squeezed him so tightly.

HOW THE SACRED PIPE WAS
BROUGHT TO THE MICMAC

Wodin'it atog'agan Glous'gapi...

USUALLY, Te'am the moose eats only plants.
His very name comes from the Micmac words
Te'a'mous'e, meaning *he strips things off trees*. But one
time long ago a giant man-eating moose began to

destroy the villages of the Micmac people. It was the very moose Glous'gap had accidentally made too large back in the days when he was busy creating the animals, and now the people were paying dearly for Glous'gap's mistake. The moose would suddenly appear when the villagers were least expecting him. With his huge hooves, the great creature would crush wigwams to the left and to the right. When men, women, and children ran screaming from their ruined homes, the moose would snatch them up in his massive jaws and chew them to bloody bits. That moose grew fat on the people's flesh. All were afraid, for every village had lost beloved relatives and friends. The elders and medicine-people held a council to determine what to do. They decided to send a messenger to Glous'gap, the powerful M'toulin or Spirit Warrior, to tell him of their plight and ask him to help.

Now when people go to seek the help of Glous'gap, they must prepare themselves for a long journey, for Glous'gap's lodge is seldom to be found in the same place. He may be camped on a reef off the coast or on a pine islet in the middle of a lake. He may be fishing on a sandy beach or hunting in the deep woods. Wherever he is, it usually takes no fewer than seven years to find him, and so it was for this messenger.

At last, the messenger found Glous'gap on the shores of a blue lake ringed with pines. As he drew near the camp, a great honking racket rose up. It was Glous'gap's flock of Canada watch-geese, sounding the alarm and warning Glous'gap of a stranger's approach.

Thanks to his loyal geese, Glous'gap was waiting to welcome the messenger into his wigwam. After they had warmed themselves by the fire and shared a pipe of tobacco, Glous'gap asked the messenger why he had come. He listened carefully to the man's story about how the Micmac lived in dread of the man-eating moose. Then Glous'gap sighed and arose, saying, "I must set things right for the people."

Glous'gap took up his maplewood bow, slung his quiver of magic arrows across his back, and led the messenger down to the lakeshore where his white canoe was beached. As they set out across the lake, Glous'gap's geese paddled in their wake, honking farewell.

Now another remarkable thing about seeking Glous'gap's help is this: though it may take seven years to find his lodge, the return journey takes but seven days, no matter how far the seeker has traveled. And so it was only a week later when the two paddled up to the messenger's village. A big crowd of people lined the shore to greet them and followed Glous'gap and the messenger to the clearing where the elders and medicine-people sat in council.

The elders had more bad news to tell. In the seven years the messenger had been gone, not only had the moose continued to ravage the land, but a second monster, a giant eagle, had joined him! This eagle had taken to swooping down on people, snatching them up in her talons, and carrying them off to his nest far to the west, where she tore them apart with her cruel beak and ate them. The Micmac were powerless against these monsters, and even the bravest trembled and glanced nervously about as the elders told these terrible things to Glous'gap.

When he had heard all, the M'toulin stood before the council and said, "I have come in answer to your prayer." Then Glous'gap prepared for battle. He painted his whole body red as blood, which our people do only when they are preparing for the most desperate combat. Then he gathered up his bow and his quiver of magic arrows and began to track the moose inland. It wasn't hard to pick up the trail, for each of the moose's hoofprints was the size of a large pond. With each great stride, the moose was heading farther and farther west.

After several days' journeying, Glous'gap at last caught up to the monster. He was standing in a large clearing, browsing on maple leaves, uprooting a whole tree with each bite and laying waste to the beautiful woodland. His dewlap was dripping with human blood, and all about him on the floor of the clearing lay the shattered bones of his victims. Now and again the moose would pause and sniff the wind in his fiery nostrils to make sure no enemy was about.

Glous'gap crouched in the shelter of a gnarled old seed-pine and studied the situation. He didn't see how he could ever manage to get within shooting range of the moose without the monster catching wind of him first. But just then a cheerful voice at his feet said, "May I help you, my brother?" It was Gopher. From the safety of his tunnel he had been watching Glous'gap size up the giant moose.

"Perhaps, little brother," Glous'gap replied. "I need a

way to sneak up on that moose so I can get close enough to shoot him."

"Good!" Gopher exclaimed. "He's always stomping around here and ruining my tunnels! I'll be glad to help you. I'll burrow right under where he's eating. Will that do?"

"Of course, little brother," Glous'gap said, and with that he made himself seven inches tall so he could fit into Gopher's tunnel. His bow and arrows shrank as well. Gopher led the way, and Glous'gap held on tightly to his friend's tail in order not to get lost in the darkness. You can still see his handprint at the tip of Gopher's tail to this day.

The burrowing seemed to take forever. The tunnel was dank and airless, and the thick odors of wet loam and leaf-mold made it hard for Glous'gap to breathe. But Gopher worked on industriously, and at last he stopped and declared, "This is the place!" Then he began to dig upward and soon popped through to the surface. Light and fresh air streamed into the tunnel, and Glous'gap was very glad to be able to see again. He and Gopher peered upward and found themselves directly under the giant moose's belly.

In all he does, Glous'gap never acts rashly. This time, even though the shot looked easy, he carefully studied the monster's underbelly. He noticed that the animal was not covered with the coarse hair of an ordinary moose. The monster moose's hide looked as if it was made out of flint or some other hard stone. Not even a magic arrow could penetrate that armor! When Glous'gap pointed this out to Gopher, the little animal scrambled out of the hole, shinnied up one of the moose's hind legs, and gnawed away the flinty hair in a circle right by the monster's heart. He was so agile and gnawed so delicately that the moose never felt him at all, and in no time Gopher was safely back in the hole.

Now Glous'gap nocked an arrow to his bow, took aim, and let fly. The flashing arrow went straight to the bald spot Gopher had made and lodged deeply in the moose's very heart.

The moose let out a thunderous bellow that echoed throughout the northern woodlands. He looked about in searing pain until he spotted the tiny figures of Glous'gap and Gopher cowering in their hole. Then he began to plow up the ground with his massive antlers, trying to get at his enemies. As the moose gouged an enormous furrow to the north, Gopher frantically began tunneling to the east. Again earth flew wildly as the moose plowed another giant furrow, this time in a northerly direction, and once again Gopher too switched directions, tunneling madly southward to escape the huge antlers. Glous'gap came right behind Gopher, pausing only to shoot more arrows into the doomed moose, until four arrows all told had found their mark in his mighty heart. Still the moose went on plowing up the ground, until he had made five vast gouges on the face of the earth. But the creature's blood was flowing freely now, and soon he dropped to the ground. With each dying breath, flecks of blood frothed from his nostrils, and at long last he lay still.

Then Glous'gap drew forth his great flint knife, sharp as a weasel's tooth, and cut off the moose's proud antlers.

Leaving the meat for Gopher, Glous'gap said goodbye to his little friend and set off for the eastern villages of the Micmac, carrying the antlers on his shoulders so he could show the people what had become of their dreaded enemy. As he loped through the woods, a huge shadow fell over him, and suddenly Glous'gap felt himself snatched up thousands of feet into the air, antlers and all! Glous'gap had forgotten all about the giant eagle. Now she had come to claim another victim. She flew off westward toward her clifftop aerie, planning to feed Glous'gap to her hungry baby eaglets.

When the eagle dropped Glous'gap into her nest, Glous'gap sprang instantly to his feet.

Using the antlers as a war club, he began to beat off the fledglings. The mother eagle circled back to help her young, and Glous'gap took a mighty swing with the antlers and crushed her skull, killing her. He scared those young eagles so badly that it stunted their growth, and that is why today there are no more giant eagles in our land.

Glous'gap climbed out of the nest and made his way down the cliff. At its foot he discovered the broken bones and torn bodies of the many people who had been carried off by the eagle. The blood of the victims had soaked into the ground and turned into a beautiful red stone. Glous'gap picked up a piece of it and fashioned it into a pipe-bowl of the sort we call *goun'dow'sen*. Then he gathered up more of the red stone and wrapped it up along with the antlers in a bundle he made from the carcass of the eagle. Once again he set off eastward, bringing the bundle back to the

Micmac villages. Upon his return, the people thronged to greet him, and they marveled when he showed them the antlers, the eagle carcass, and the red stone.

"From now on you need never fear the moose or the eagle," Glous'gap told the people. "This red stone is the blood of your ancestors. From it, you will make pipes. This pipe is sacred. It is your altar, and you will carry it with you wherever you go. The pipestem of white ash is your backbone. Tobacco shall be your offering, and the smoke is your prayers rising. When you use this pipe to make your prayers, do it in a sacred manner and your prayers will be answered. If you use it wrongly, harm will come back on you and your families. Use the pipe wisely. Be careful of what you pray for, because you will get exactly what you ask for."

That is the story of how Glous'gap conquered the giant moose and the giant eagle and in doing so brought the sacred pipe to the Micmac. The truth of the story is written on the face of the land. If you look at a map of North America, you can see the five huge gouges the frantic moose made in the earth. Today, they are filled up with water, and people call them the Great Lakes. Farther west, in the southwest corner of Minnesota, lies the site of the giant eagle's nest, where the blood of our ancestors turned to stone. Today it is called Pipestone National Monument, and Native American peoples from all across the continent come there for stone to make their pipes, just like the first pipe Glous'gap made for us so long ago.

GLOUS'GAP AND
PAINTED TURTLE

Wodin'it atog'agan Glous'gapi...

L ONG AGO, Glous'gap lived for a time among
our people in a large village near Grand Lake,
in what is now the province of New Brunswick. It
was a beautiful place surrounded by tall shade trees.

Every morning the women would sweep the ground around their lodges with pine or spruce boughs to keep the village clean.

In the neatest wigwam of the whole village Glous'gap dwelled with Mrs. Bear, whom he called Nou'goum'i, or Grandmother. Our people say that Glous'gap was sent among us to teach us the right way in which to live, and to be sure, Mrs. Bear was just like him. She was a wise and generous old woman who was always helping out people in need and teaching the girls and younger women all the special things they needed to know.

In those days a man called Painted Turtle lived across the village in a wigwam all by himself. He didn't have a wife of his own, but he fancied himself quite the ladies' man. He would flirt with any woman who would look at him, and quite a few women did so, in spite of their better judgment, because he was such a handsome and smooth-talking fellow. No doubt about it, Painted Turtle had the power to lure women, and thus he stole girls away from their sweethearts and wives away from their husbands and made trouble for everyone in the village.

Finally the whole town was in such an uproar of gossip and jealousy and fear and broken hearts that Mrs. Bear said to Glous'gap in exasperation, "You've got to do something about that rascally Painted Turtle! Nobody can get anything done because of him. The men won't go out hunting because they're afraid to leave their wives alone in the village with him, and the women won't go out to gather plants for food or wood for their cooking fires because they're afraid he'll follow them into the forest and practice his wiles on them. You were sent here to help the people learn to live happily and at peace with one another, and so it's up to you to put a stop to this business!"

"All right," replied Glous'gap, "I will."

Drawing upon his magic, Glous'gap turned himself into a slender young woman with long shining black hair, full lips, and soft brown eyes like a doe's. Then Glous'gap-woman picked up a wooden bowl of corn soup that was steaming by the fire and walked with a lightly swaying gait across the encampment until she came to the lodge of Painted Turtle. "Hello! Here I am," she called out in a low musical voice. "I've brought you a gift!"

Painted Turtle sat as he always did, with the entrance flap of his lodge wide open so he could spy on people passing by. Of course he especially had his eye out for women, and he was a little flustered by this lovely stranger who had come to his lodge of her own accord and now stood outside calling to him. His lustful heart raged, and he quickly began to scheme how he might best have his way with her. "Come in," he called out, once he'd decided on one of his tried and proven methods of seduction.

Smiling shyly, her eyes downcast, Glous'gap-woman stepped through the door of the birchbark-covered lodge. Turtle was lounging on his bed, leaning back against a log and carefully painting his face. He daubed a red dot on each cheek and made a big red dot right in the center of his forehead. Then he parted his hair down the middle with a maplewood stick and painted the part red, too. Suddenly, he turned aside and spat into the fire. His spittle turned into a freshwater pearl-and-shell *up'kous'un*, or necklace.

"Go ahead, pick it up!" said Painted Turtle to his shy guest, waving his hand nonchalantly toward the gleaming necklace. "There's plenty more where that one came from!" Glous'gap-woman knelt and gingerly gathered up the necklace from the blackened stones that ringed the fire.

Turtle went on to paint a broad red line around one leg, and when he was done he spat into the fire again. This time the spittle magically turned into an iridescent choker made of *oul'nap'skouk*, or wampum shell. While Glous'gap-woman plucked it from the fire and held it to the light to admire it, Turtle busied himself painting a red line around his other leg. When he spat into the fire a third time, a matching set of shell earrings appeared. "Those are for you too, my dear," said Turtle casually. "And if you'll only come for a walk with me in the woods, I'll have something even better to give you. I know all the secrets of the forest!"

"Oh dear, I just don't think I ought to go walking alone in the woods with any man," said Glous'gap-woman. She looked longingly at the gifts and turned them over and over in her slender hands, as if enchanted by their beauty. "My grandmother says that is how girls always get into trouble."

"Look at me!" commanded Turtle, in a voice that suggested his feelings were deeply hurt. "Don't you think I'm handsome? Don't you like the way I look, now that I've gone to all the trouble of painting myself just for you? Do you think a man like me would ever try to cause a woman trouble?" He shook his head sadly, as if in disbelief that Glous'gap-woman could have gotten such a wrong impression of him.

"Well, I don't know," said Glous'gap-woman hesitantly, still turning the jewelry over and over in her hands. Now it looked as though she were thinking about taking that walk in the woods with Painted Turtle after all. That little bit of hesitancy was just what Painted Turtle was looking for, and now he began to press her harder. He really wanted to get this beautiful strange woman alone.

"Oh, come on, now," he insisted, taking her by the elbow. "I'll show you all sorts of things!"

"Well, I guess it will be all right," said Glous'gap-woman meekly, and she let Painted Turtle lead her out of his wigwam and into the shadows of the woods.

The couple walked on for a long way, admiring the mocassin-flowers and the ghostly white Indian pipes and all the different kinds of mushrooms that Painted Turtle pointed out growing in the leafy mulch of the forest floor. At last the path they were following led them to a small clearing. The tree branches arched overhead and shaded it, just as if it were a summer brush-shelter.

"Here we are!" exclaimed Painted Turtle happily, as he sat down and leaned back against the broad trunk of a tree. He patted the ground next to him. "Come sit here beside me, my little sweetheart!" he called.

Glous'gap-woman gazed wide-eyed around the little clearing and then cautiously sat herself down beside Painted Turtle. He slipped his arm around her. "There, isn't this nice, now?" he asked. Then he pretended to yawn, and gradually he eased himself down until he was lying flat on his back. "Come on, why not just lie back and take a little rest, my dear? You must be so very tired after that long walk!" he said in a soothing voice as he stroked her shoulder.

Glous'gap-woman obediently lay down beside Painted Turtle. He drew her close to him, murmuring in her ear about her beauty and how glad he was they could be alone together in this romantic place just meant for the two of them. Glous'gap-woman stared up at him in wonder, as if she were spellbound by his sweet talk. Painted Turtle closed his eyes dreamily—and within seconds, he was sound asleep and snoring! Glous'gap-woman was the one casting the stronger spell, and sure enough, she had charmed Painted Turtle into a deep slumber.

Then Glous'gap-woman sprang up and looked about until she spied a rotten log in the underbrush at the edge of the clearing. The log was swarming with red ants, the kind that can kill if a person is bitten by too many of them. Glous'gap-woman rolled the log over to where Painted Turtle lay. Out of his dreaming, the would-be lover sighed, "Oh, my little sweetheart," and sleepily threw his arms around the log and hugged it. The ants, angry at their home being disturbed, began to crawl all over Painted Turtle's body. "Don't do that!" mumbled Turtle. "You tickle!" He was still very drowsy and could not seem to open his eyes. The ants kept crawling over him, swarming out of their log in even greater numbers. "Lie still!" he ordered. "You can't find out about the secrets I brought you here to show you if you keep on tickling me!" and he began to thrash about.

By this time, the ants were angry enough to begin biting him. At that, Painted Turtle bolted upright and discovered he had been hugging a rotten log. He started slapping at the ants in astonishment and looked wildly about for his lovely young companion. There in the clearing stood the mighty Glous'gap, restored to his own form.

"Painted Turtle," said Glous'gap sternly, "you've caused trouble for this village long enough. From now on, you will crawl on your belly to pay for all your wrongdoing, and I'm going to leave all your gaudy paint showing on you, too. By those fancy red dots and streaks, everyone will know you for who and what you are!"

And so it was that Glous'gap transformed that irresponsible young man into the painted turtle we see around our ponds and streams today. Glous'gap did what his grandmother bade him, and made things come out right. Ever after, when our young men behold the painted turtle crawling on his belly and showing his bright red body-paint, they remember that they must not act toward women as Painted Turtle did. Instead, they resolve to cherish women as sisters and friends, as cousins and aunts, as daughters and wives and mothers.

THE BOY IN THE
BIRCHBARK BOX

Wodin'it atog'agan Glous'gapi . . .

GLOUS'GAP in his many travels once happened upon a hunting camp far in the north woods. There he found a man and his wife grieving. "What is wrong, my friends?" he asked. "Why do you weep so?"

The couple looked at each other in despair and then turned to Glous'gap. "Our son has run away," they told him. "He says he hates us, and despises his very name! He resents everything we ask him to do, even when it is only to gather firewood or to go hunting! He says he hates his lot in life and deplores the way we treat him."

Glous'gap puzzled about this, especially when he learned the boy was only twelve winters old. How could he hate these good parents, and indeed his whole life, with so little knowledge of the world?

"Where is your son?" Glous'gap asked. "In what direction did he set off?"

"We didn't see him go," the father sighed. "All we know is that he's gone, and he's taken a bow and some arrows, the new pair of mocassins his mother just made him, and my canoe. We can't think what to do! He is our only child, and we have tried so hard to love him well and bring him up right."

Glous'gap stayed with the heartbroken family all that night to console them, but by the time the sun rose from beneath the earth on the following morning he realized the only way to ease their pain would be to bring their son safely home to them.

Stepping outside the wigwam, Glous'gap drew one of his arrows from his quiver. He nocked that arrow to his bow, aimed it skyward, and let it fly. Of course it was a magic arrow, and he knew that whatever direction it took, that would be the way the boy had fled. Glous'gap ran after the arrow's unswerving arc until he came to the place where it had fallen. He snatched it up and shot it aloft again, once more following its unerring path. Glous'gap did this many times until he began to feel at one with the arrow. Soon he was outrunning it, catching it in midair, and shooting it forth again without once breaking his stride. His power was mounting, and he could sense the boy's trail growing warmer. By nightfall, he was far from the camp of the sorrowful parents.

"Where's that boy gotten to, eh?" he said aloud. But no answer came because the dark itself has no voice, and therefore Glous'gap asked no more.

For seven days Glous'gap tracked the youngster, stopping every night to rest. In all that time he saw no sign of a camp or a footprint or even a fire. Still, he did not give up hope. He knew his arrow would guide him true, and he resolved to be patient.

Meantime, what had happened to the runaway boy? He was voyaging far down river in his stolen canoe when he spied an old man hailing him from the bank.

"*Tami'a'lin?* Where are you going?" the elder called.

The boy did not want to be pinned down, so he answered evasively. "I've paddled a far distance," he replied. "And you, *nigsgam'itj,* my grandfather? Have you traveled far?"

"Oh, I've come a ways," said the old man.

Now, the boy did not know it, but this was really no kindly grandfather who stood there before him, doddering about in his worn moccasins and smiling his broken-toothed smile. Oh, no—it was none other than the witch

Poug'tjin'skwes herself in one of her many shadowy guises, and she was out that day to capture another victim in order to gain more power for her wicked sorceries.

"Do you have room in your canoe for an elder like me?" wheedled Poug'tjin'skwes, sounding like the nicest old man you could imagine. "We seem to be going in the same direction. Besides, two on the paddles will make for better time, eh?"

The boy had to admit that was true, and he pulled up close to the embankment so the kindly old fellow could climb into the *kwi'den*. But as soon as the elder stepped into the canoe, all his old-man disguise seemed to fall away into tatters at his feet, and Poug'tjin'skwes appeared to the boy as a slavering she-hag. The sorceress reached out and seized him with her gnarled hand. She clutched the startled youngster by the wrist and sang an incantation that caused him to shrink until he was no bigger than her thumb. Then she caught him up and popped him into the sort of small birchbark box we call a *mag'gak* and fastened the lid down tight.

When the boy shrank so abruptly, the moccasins the boy's mother had lovingly sewn and beaded for him were left standing empty, side by side on the floor of the canoe. "Oh ho! I get new moccasins out of this, too!" Poug'tjin'skwes cackled as she reached for the pair. "Oh, what a fine gift!" she mocked as she slipped them on her bony feet. "Thank you, thank you, *nou'tjitj*, my grandchild!" Then she snatched up the *mag'gak*, flipped opened the lid, and peered inside. All the terrified boy could see was one enormous eye of Poug'tjen'skwes leering down at him. Delighted with her victory, she had assumed her true form as a beautiful woman, but the boy did not think of her as beautiful. He sobbed, longing for his own mother's soft voice and the warmth of her arms. He wished for his father's strength and steadiness. Poug'tjin'skwes just laughed and shook the box a little. The boy could only cling to a deer-sinew seam that ran up one side.

"What is this I see?" cooed the witch. "Why, what do you know? There's a tiny boy inside this box! A little tiny boy drenched in sweat and quaking with fear!"

The boy covered his eyes with one arm and reached the other out toward her in supplication. "What do you want?" he pleaded. "Why have you done this to me?"

"What is it you want? Why have you done this to me?" mocked the witch in a squeaky voice. Her eyes darkened and narrowed as she squinted down at the youngster huddled in a corner of the box. "Why," she said, grinning horribly, "all I want is your tiny little *manitou*, your spirit, your soul, so I can feed my power!"

"Oh," the boy cried, burying his head in his hands, "I wish I'd never left my parents and our lodge! I wish I'd stayed where I was safe, and people cared about me!"

"Too late now! Stop your whining!" Poug'tjin'skwes sneered as she slammed the cover down on the *mag'gak*. Once again darkness engulfed the boy. He fainted and slumped to the bottom of the birchbark box.

Time passed. When the boy awoke, he found himself secured to a basswood sapling by a leather thong.

Gathering his wits, he looked around him and saw the hugely beautiful and cruel Poug'tjen'skwes grinning at him. He shuddered to realize that his captivity had not just been a menacing dream. It was all true. He was three inches tall, and he was in the merciless hands of Poug'tjin'skwes.

Just at that moment, when the boy was sunk in despair, Glous'gap came bounding into the camp, spun around, and deftly snatched from mid-air his magic arrow. He knew he had finally come to the place where the runaway was living, though he could not see him. He stopped, looked about, and called out his greeting: *Tou'lada'doul dim' kewe!*

Poug'tjin'skwes recognized him right away and instantly transformed herself into a pitiable old crone. Snaking her arm out, she shoved the tiny boy under the birchbark box and clapped it upside-down. Then she rose on trembling limbs to welcome Glous'gap into her camp. "Come, my grandson, and sit in the place of honor, up here behind the fire!" she said in her quavery voice. "I'm weak and suffering, but I'll try to cook something nice for you to eat!" As soon as Glous'gap sat down, the hag began to cry.

"Why are you weeping, *Nou'gou'mitj*, my grandmother?" Glous'gap asked solicitously.

"Ah, *Nou'tjitj*, my grandson, what's an old woman to do?" she answered, dabbing at her eyes. "I am alone in this world. My husband is dead these many years, and I am so old! I hear many strange sounds coming from the woods at night. Spirits call out to me from the land of shadows, and I have not slept for many nights for fear they may overtake me. Dear *Nou'tjitj*, will you watch over an old woman, so she may sleep through one night in peace? All I ask is that you stand guard until sunrise."

Now Glous'gap had recognized Poug'tjin'skwes as soon as he came running into her camp, but he was not about to reveal that. "I'll watch over you carefully, *Nou'goum'itj!*" he vowed, and he smiled to himself, knowing he was telling no lie.

Poug'tjin'skwes lay down beneath the stolen canoe and covered herself over with a deerhide blanket. As she watched the fire die down to embers, her eyes grew heavy in spite of herself, and soon she was truly asleep. Glous'gap had used his magic to put her into a deep slumber. Then he quickly surveyed the campsite.

At first, nothing seemed out of place. The night was still except for the steady gurgle of the river and Poug'tjin'-skwes' snores. Then Glous'gap heard a small muffled voice. "*A'bo'goun'um'we! Help me!*" the voice pleaded. Glous'gap searched the camp by the embers' glow to discover where the voice came from. At last he spied the overturned *mag'-gak* with a *ba'bitj*, a leather thong, running out from beneath it and tethered to the basswood sapling.

Hunkering down to get a closer look, Glous'gap gently lifted the lid of the *mag'gak*. When he did, he could see the trapped boy secured at the other end of the thong. Glous'-gap delicately picked up the little fellow and held him between finger and thumb to examine his find. "Why, you're the one I've been looking for!" Glous'gap exclaimed. "But nobody ever told me you'd be so small!"

The boy wept, "That witch has done this to me! She's

penned me up in this *mag'gak* to use me for her sorcery, but all I want to do is to go home to my parents. Please help me, please!"

Glous'gap glanced over at Poug'tjin'skwes and then stared gravely at the little one who now stood trembling in the palm of his hand. "All right. I will do this. I will get you home safely," he assured the boy. He gingerly scooped him back into the birchbark box, and tucking box and boy into his *up'sakum'ote*, his medicine pouch, he quietly stole away from Poug'tjin'skwes' camp.

The morning sun was already slanting brightly down on her face when Poug'tjin'skwes started awake, wrapped in her deerskin blanket beneath the canoe. She looked anxiously about her, trying to remember what had happened the night before. Somehow she had fallen asleep and not gotten around to working her evil upon her enemy Glous'-gap. And speaking of Glous'gap, where was he? She'd expected to see him stupidly tending the fire and keeping watch, but he was nowhere to be found, nor was the upside-down *mag'gak* with the tiny boy tethered within.

In her rage, Poug'tjin'skwes shrieked like a wounded creature and ran deep into the forest. Snuffing at the ground and spying tracks, she picked up the trail of Glous'gap and pursued him hotly, baying, "I'll flay the meat from your bones! I'll cut off your head and hang it from a pole for all to see! I'll grind your very bones to dust! And you think you have outwitted me, *me, ME?*"

Glous'gap could hear her bellowing and thrashing through the underbrush on his back trail, and although she was still some distance behind him, he could tell she was gaining on him. He dashed up a granite mountainside blanketed with fir, spruce and pine, then sprinted over the top and down the other side until he came to a glimmering lake teeming with fish. At the water's edge, gray rock ledges extended well out from the sandy shore. Glous'gap had just made it to the farthest point of one ledge when the ravening Poug'tjin'skwes broke through the treeline.

"Give back what is mine!" she screeched out to Glous'gap.

"*Mo'kwe*—No!" Glous'gap called back defiantly. "This boy does not belong to you! I will never hand him over!"

"Just tell him to come to me!" Poug'tjin'skwes wailed.

"Never!" replied the mighty M'toulin.

Poug'tjin'skwes was infuriated, but she figured she had trapped Glous'gap and his tiny passenger at the end of the ledge, and she called up all her powers. Howling, twisting, and thrashing, she transformed herself into a *tji'pitj'gam*, the sort of giant horned serpent-being that haunts deep lakes. Intent upon killing Glous'gap, she slithered forward on her bloated belly until she was near enough to rear up over him like a massive *tas'goum*, or snake. Glous'gap did not try to run forward and attack her, as she had hoped. Instead he waited for her to draw even closer. She hissed at him, "This time, there's no escape for you!"

But Glous'gap just said, "Well, we shall see," and with that he vaulted into the air and landed, gripping the she-serpent's neck with his knees, just behind her hissing head.

Glous'gap grappled to hold his seat as Poug'tjin'skwes

pitched herself sideways and up and down in her efforts to throw him from her back. Glous'gap strained forward to reach the two spiraling horns that grew from her forehead. He finally got a grasp upon one of them and swung himself up and clung there. Despite her pitching and yawing, he managed to scrape some powder off the horn with his fingernails, and he brushed it into his medicine bag, where the boy still clung to the sides of the birchbark box.

Poug'tjin'skwes thrashed around mightily in her efforts to dislodge Glous'gap. Her scaly tail toppled trees for miles about the lake as it swept to and fro, but nothing could unseat the young M'toulin. To her dismay he roared with laughter as he whipped around on that wild ride, and he cried out, "Is this the best you can do, oh most powerful and grand witch that you are? You say you'll flay meat from my bones, hang my head from a pole, and grind my very bones to dust? Why, you are nothing but the unpleasant wind that comes after a greasy meal!"

At last Poug'tjin'skwes collapsed on the ledge in exhaustion. As she slumped forward Glous'gap leaped from her neck, and Poug'tjin'skwes' body began to return to its true form. The little waves of the lake lapped over her. Now she simply looked like any woman lying there in the shallows with a scowl on her face.

Glous'gap fished the birchbark box out of his medicine pouch and opened it so the runaway boy could crawl out. Then he poured the powder he'd scraped from the horn of the *tji'pitj'gam* into his palm, and blew that dust over the boy's body. Once covered with that magical powder, the boy was restored to his normal size. Glous'gap laid his hand on the boy's shoulder and motioned that they should begin to walk back along the river, toward the stolen canoe. The boy looked fearfully over at Poug'tjin'skwes, but she only lay where she had fallen, glaring after them, too humiliated and too weary to give chase.

Glous'gap escorted the boy back upriver to his parents, who rejoiced to see him. He was ever after a good son, and in time he became a kind husband and father and a praiseworthy hunter. If ever he felt a little impatient or dissatisfied with his lot, he always recalled the time he had spent as a boy in a birchbark box, and he shuddered and gave thanks for his life.

GLOUS'GAP AND WOTJOU'SAN, THE WIND BIRD

Wodin'it atog'agan Glous'gapi ...

ONCE IN THE TIME of our ancestors a giant bird of prey called Wotjou'san used to swoop down from the north on the villages of our people. Each time he came he carried off some poor unsuspecting man, woman, or child and winged his way back to his nest, where he would tear his victims limb from limb and eat them. That bird would descend upon a village so unexpectedly there was never time to take cover, and the people lived in constant dread of him. At last the chiefs, the elders, and the medicine people held a great council and determined to send a messenger to seek the help of Glous'gap, the Lord of Beasts and Human Beings.

Always when people seek out Glous'gap they must be prepared for a long and arduous journey, and so it was with the man the council chose for their messenger. He traveled for seven years and endured many hardships before he found Glous'gap. When he was still three months' journey from the Holy One's camp, he could already hear the riotous honking sent up by Glous'gap's flock of watch-geese. When the messenger finally reached the camp by a lake far inland, Glous'gap raised his hand to silence the geese. He seated his weary guest on a white bearskin, and together they shared a quiet smoke from Glous'gap's stone-bowl pipe. Then the man told Glous'gap about the trouble the people were having with the bird from the north country. "I will help," said Glous'gap, as he gathered up his bow and his quiver of arrows, and together the two set out for the villages where fearful people cowered, constantly listening for the terrible rush of wings that would mean Wotjou'san had come again. As always, the return trip took only seven days, much to the surprise of the messenger, who was still bone-tired from his seven-year quest after Glous'gap.

Glous'gap left the messenger at his home village and

set off north through deep woods. He knew right away where he must go. He passed through the Micmac villages of the Gaspé and waded across the Saint Lawrence, the great river that leads to the Big Waters of the East. He left behind him the villages of the northern relatives, the Naskapi and the Eastern Cree, and made his way far into the north country, where it is barren and always covered with snows. At last he came to a boulder-strewn mountain, and he began to climb it. Along the lower slopes he discovered the scattered bones of many people, and the stench of death filled his nostrils. He choked at the smell, but he knew he must be near the nest of the giant bird. At last he found what he was looking for, a hollowed-out place the size of a whole mountain valley, crudely lined with brush and tree-limbs the giant bird had gathered far to the south. Wotjou'san was nowhere in sight, so Glous'gap hunkered down behind a huge granite boulder at the rim of the nest to wait for the monster's return.

All at once a deep shadow fell across the mountain, and a terrible wind struck Glous'gap with freezing blasts. When he looked up, he could see the bird beating his wings, coming in for a landing. Each wingfeather was as long as the tallest pine tree, and with each stroke of those giant wings, a fresh gale blew. Glous'gap clung to the boulder for dear life, trying to keep from being blown off the mountain. The wind shredded all of his clothing to nothing, and as Wotjou'san drew yet nearer, that wind even blew the very hair off Glous'gap's head! Naked and bald, poor Glous'gap squinted his eyes shut and pressed his body closely to the granite surface as the icy wind knifed around him.

With a great flurry of feathers, the bird landed and settled himself in his nest. He turned his head from side to side and surveyed the countryside with his huge yellow eyes, but he could not see Glous'gap crouching behind the boulder at the very rim of the nest.

No one can say exactly how long Glous'gap remained hidden, but the night was already hours old before he dared to leave the cover of the boulder. By that time the Arctic moon had risen and now it bathed all in its cold silver light. Peering over the edge of the nest, Glous'gap could see that the great bird was asleep, his head tucked beneath his wing. Wotjou'san stirred a little in his sleep, as though he might be dreaming of hunting delicious man-flesh. Working quickly and quietly, Glous'gap took up his bow made of maplewood, whose bowstring is the rainbow. He unstrung it and looped the shimmering rainbow cord like a lasso in his hands. Then he lowered himself into the nest and trussed the feet and wings of the monster bird so that he could neither run nor flap.

"Wotjou'san!" Glous'gap called out loudly. "Wake up, Wotjou'san, and behold the one who has tamed you!" His voice echoed and rolled around the huge hollow of the nest. Wotjou'san's yellow eyes flew open, and his terrible shriek of anger rent the wintery night. The bird searched madly about until he spied the naked, bald, and grinning figure of Glous'gap standing with his hands on his hips on the edge of his very nest. Wotjou'san tried to hurl himself at Glous'gap, and it was then he discovered he was powerless to move. He began to stab at Glous'gap with his fearsome sharp beak, but Glous'gap only leaped lightly out of the way, laughing and taunting. Then he began his long trek back to the villages of our people. Behind him, he could still hear the bird's shrill cries of rage.

The long journey home gave Glous'gap a chance to regrow his hair, and on the way he also shot a deer and made fine new clothes for himself out of buckskin. By the time he was safely back at the village, Glous'gap looked like himself once again. He told all the people about his conquest of Wotjou'san, and there was much feasting, rejoicing, singing, and speechifying. All the people were sure their troubles were over, and they smiled to think of the monster bird bound up tightly in his mountain aerie far to the north. When the celebrations were done, Glous'gap said his farewells and set out for his own lodge far inland. "Well, that's that," he thought to himself, as he looked back over his shoulder at the people waving goodbye. But even Glous'gap is sometimes wrong.

In the villages all went well for a few months, until the people began to notice that something was amiss with the waters of their land. The brooks and the lakes and even the big salt waters of the east began to foul. An ugly yellow scum gathered atop the waters. Fish gasped at the surface and then turned belly-up and died, and the riverbanks and the seashores were strewn with their bloated corpses. A pall lay over the land, and no breeze came to blow away the dreadful smell. The people grew sick from the smell and the lack of fresh water. Once again they called a high council, and once again a messenger made his arduous way to Glous'gap's lodge. Once again the great watch-geese announced his arrival, and once again Glous'gap welcomed the guest, offered him the pipe, and listened to what he had to say. When he learned about the dying sea and fetid waterways, he grew solemn indeed.

Glous'gap gathered the people of all the villages together and said "This *ko'gan*, this scum, is forming because there's no wind. Wait here, and I'll set things right." Then Glous'gap made the difficult journey northward all over again. At last he came to the boulder-strewn mountain, and he climbed to the nest where Wotjou'san lay trussed up tightly with the length of rainbow cord. "Easy, now, " Glous'gap soothed as he unbound one of the bird's great wings.

As soon as the wing was freed, the bird set up a mighty flapping, and a cold wind blew strongly southward across the land, toward the villages of our people. It stirred the lakes, the streams, and the Big Waters of the East, freshening them, and soon the waters were clear of the yellow scum. Once again salmon and alewives swam crazily upstream during their spring runs. Fat trout lazed in dappled woodland pools, and the sea teemed with cod and striped bass and halibut. With one wing, Wotjou'san made just enough wind to keep the waters clean, and Glous'gap smiled to see the world once again restored to balance.

GLOUS'GAP AND THE
LITTLE SUMMER WOMAN

Wodin'it atog'agan Glous'gapi . . .

IN THE LONG AGO TIME when Glous'gap
walked among the ancestors, a giant named Kesik
lived in the north country. When he shook his great
hoary head, snow came tumbling from his hair and

covered the mountains, the forests, the valleys, and the sea-coast for thousands of miles with eye-blinding whiteness. One huff of his frosty breath turned water into ice harder than any stone. In the giant's presence, the land grew so cold that boulders split in two. Huge trees cracked apart, and their limbs shattered like glass as they hit the ground. The birds and animals froze dead in their tracks in the middle of whatever they were doing, and soon the snowy woodlands were filled with what seemed to be statues of rabbits hopping, deer browsing, and crows cawing silently from snow-laden branches. All grew deathly still except for the sound of the whistling wind, and thus our broad red land was turned into a white frozen desolation.

Our people suffered through this harsh time. When someone set his *wis'koug'wow* or cookpot on the fire to boil, one side would grow warm while the other side facing the door flap remained frozen hard. Nobody dared to leave the wigwam except to gather more wood for the fire, and even wood-gathering was done at the risk of one's very life.

Now Glous'gap knows everything that goes on in the world even before it happens. He knew what the people were going through, and he could guess what being must be causing this terrible cold. Glous'gap prepared himself to do battle with Kesik, the winter giant. He gathered up a bearskin and his maplewood bow and his arrows, the ones that always find their mark and then magically return themselves to their owner's quiver. When Glous'gap lifted the entrance flap of his lodge, the icy breath of Kesik caused his lungs to ache. The wind sliced right through him and numbed his limbs. Glous'gap wrapped his bearskin tighter around him and peered about. The *wast'ow*, the snow, lay drifted waist-high in all directions. "I'll need my snowshoes if I'm to travel any distance through this stuff," said Glous'gap to himself, as the freezing wind sucked his breath right out of him. He tucked moss and dry grass into his moccasins to keep his feet from frostbite, and tied his *ag'am'oug* onto the mocassins. Then he leaned into the wind with tremendous resolve and began to fight his way toward its source.

Glous'gap's journey took many days. It was eerie to snowshoe past the frozen animals and the shattered trees, all drifted over with snow. With whiteness blanketing all, it was hard to tell directions, but Glous'gap just kept facing straight into the icy wind, for he felt sure it was the breath that came straight from the lungs of Kesik. At last Glous'gap came to the giant's encampment. It stood in a clearing surrounded by the skeletal remains of ruined trees. Everything was coated with snow and ice, and no color but white could be seen.

Glous'gap knew this was a place of death. Nonetheless he strode boldly across the clearing and scratched at the frozen hide-flap that covered the entrance of the lodge. "*Come in!*" boomed a deep loud voice from within. Glous'gap politely removed his snowshoes and slipped inside the enormous snow-covered wigwam. There beside the smallest fire imaginable sat a giant with a great mane of snow-white hair and bushy eyebrows rimed with ice. He motioned with one hand for Glous'gap to be seated on a white bearskin near the fire. Glous'gap sat down, but he was careful never to take his eyes off his hoary host.

Kesik rummaged through a huge pouch made from the whole hide of a caribou and fished out an enormous pipe that he promptly filled with tobacco and handed over to Glous'gap. As Glous'gap smoked the pipe, the giant began to tell him tales of the olden times, when all the world was locked in winter and sheets of ice as tall as mountains pushed and groaned their way southward. In those days, Kesik said, strange beasts roamed the earth. In his slow, deep voice he went on to tell stories of animals with tough hairy hides, snaky trunks, and long tusks, and tales of dreadful cats with curving incisors as long as a man's forearm. Kesik sounded as though he missed those olden days very much. Glous'gap puffed away at the pipe and listened dreamily, imagining the beauty of the shining blue-white ice and the great beasts who dwelt in that long-ago world of endless winter.

Now all the while Kesik unfolded these tales of wonder, a mist gradually arose around Glous'gap. It hovered about him for a while, and then it slowly settled upon him like hoarfrost and covered his whole body over with a white rime. Soon he fell sound asleep. Kesik had used the magic of his breath and his stories against Glous'gap, and even the Lord of Beasts and Human Beings had succumbed to that wintery spell. Then Glous'gap slept for six whole months, just as if he were a toad or a frog who had tunneled into mud to hibernate.

When the magic at last began to wear off, Glous'gap awoke and found himself alone in a dismal frozen bog. The deep sleep left him feeling confused and thick-headed, with no clear sense of direction. All he knew for sure was that he had a powerful desire to head for home. Placing one foot in front of the other, he wandered aimlessly for a long time. When he finally came back to himself, he looked around and realized he must have bypassed his own lodge. He seemed to be someplace to the south of his homeland, and with every step he took it grew warmer. Melting snow dripped musically from the tree limbs, and wider and wider patches of muddy ground appeared at his feet. After a while the buds began to swell on the trees, and the first tender green grasses and early plants sprang up out of the mud—the smelly skunk cabbage, tightly curled fiddlehead ferns, the jack-in-the-pulpit, the moccasin flower, and the little white snowdrop. Glous'gap greeted them all, glad for their company, and they began to speak to him. "Keep heading south," they told him, and their advice pleased him. He had endured enough winter to last him a long while.

Glous'gap journeyed far to the south, across plains and basins, across great rivers and mountain ranges higher than he had ever seen. At last he came to a village of the Summer people. These folk were smaller than the Micmac. They welcomed him warmly, and as they shared their strange food with him, he watched them dance. They did not dance in a circle around a fire, as we usually do, with our musicians off to one side around a big drum. Instead, they danced first in two long parallel lines, one of men and one of women. After a while the men and women formed pairs and danced in a single long line. Finally the whole tribe of Summer people danced as one in a circle around a group of drummers and singers who shook gourd rattles.

The drummers beat out their strong rhythms on deerhide drums small enough for a man to carry as he walked about.

Soon Glous'gap's attention was drawn to a certain woman among the dancers. Her black hair fell down her back as straight as rain, and her bare brown feet moved gracefully across the dusty earth of the dancing place. Glous'gap believed she must be the most beautiful woman who had ever been born. He rose and joined the line of male dancers until he found himself dancing just opposite to her. Then he caught her up and swiftly ran away with her, covering great distances with each mighty stride.

Of course the Summer people pursued him, but Glous'gap had a plan to foil them. He cut a moosehide into a long cord strip, and he played it out behind him with one hand as he ran, carrying the little Summer Woman in his other arm. When the Summer people came upon Glous'gap's moosehide cord, they naturally stopped and began to pull on it, thinking to rein Glous'gap up short and then reel him back toward them. But the cord was not fastened to Glous'gap and so it simply ran out, and Glous'gap left his pursuers far behind, holding only the empty end. They called after him in their own language, crying "Stop, Long Sash, stop! Come back!" But Glous'gap kept on running toward the North Country. He cradled the little Summer Woman in his arms, carrying her close to his chest. As they neared the North, he stopped to wrap her warmly in a bearskin. She did not try to fight him, for Glous'gap had used his magic to make her fall into a peaceful sleep.

When at last Glous'gap came once more to the lodge

of Kesik, the giant welcomed his visitor eagerly, for he hoped to freeze Glous'gap right back into sleep again. Glous'gap ducked through the flap into the snowy lodge, still carrying the little Summer Woman hidden under his robes, and he smiled agreeably and sat himself down by the fire. Again the winter giant brought out his great pipe, filled it with tobacco, and lit it. But this time as they smoked it was Glous'gap who did all the talking. He told Kesik about his journey. In a slow, warm voice he told of the sun and the smell of summer rain on sun-baked earth. He spoke about strange foods that tasted of the sun's heat, and he told how an entire village would dance in two long lines, one of men and one of women, there in the land where summer seems never to end. As Glous'gap talked on, one drop of sweat and then another popped out on Kesik's forehead. Soon he was wringing wet, but still Glous'gap's voice held him in thrall.

There in Glous'gap's arms the little Summer Woman slept on. She softly sighed in her sleep and she smiled as she felt the icy cold begin to abate. Out of her dreaming she began to sing a Summer Song of magical power. The warmth of her song made Kesik melt even faster. His wigwam of ice and snow started to collapse, and soon it lay in a slushy heap. *A'io!* Yes, Kesik's whole winter world was melting fast, and at last he regained command of himself and did the only thing left for him to do. Trailing his soggy fur robes, he fled to the farthest part of the North Country, where he still lives today.

Soon everything awoke from the winter spell. The grasses grew, the trees budded, all the spring flowers burst into bloom, and the birds and animals unfroze and continued about their busy lives. The melting snow ran down the channels of the rivers and carried away the dead leaves and the broken branches, and all was again as it should be.

Glous'gap returned the little Summer Woman to her people far to the south. When they saw that she was unharmed, they were no longer angry at Glous'gap. He left her among them and made the Summer people promise to journey up to the northlands every year. And they have kept their promise to Glous'gap ever since.

GLOUS'GAP
AND THE GULLS

Wodin'it atog'agan Glous'gapi . . .

ONE SUMMER GLOUS'GAP decided to visit
a band of folk who lived near the mouth of
the Apple River in Nova Scotia. They called themselves the Deer people on account of a special dance

they did before they went hunting, a dance that drew the deer into easy range of their bows and arrows. Glous'gap wanted to see this dance for himself because he'd heard it was very strong medicine indeed. So it was that he set forth in his magic white canoe to visit the Deer people and share in their preparations for the hunt.

When he beached before their village in the late afternoon, the Deer people came down to the shore to welcome him. Leading the party was a beautiful young woman who introduced herself as their *sagama*, or chief. Now there have always been women *sagamas* among us, so Glous'gap was not surprised that the Deer people's chief should be a slender woman with gleaming black hair. But as she drew closer Glous'gap recognized through that lovely disguise the evil witch Poug'tjin'skwes, his old enemy. He remembered how over the years Poug'tjin'skwes in her many shape-shiftings had often tried to do him in with spells and tricks and poisons.

Glous'gap never let on that he recognized the she-fiend. Instead he greeted her and the Deer people warmly. He let them lead him into their village, and they feasted him all that evening on clams and venison and corn soup. Glous'gap smiled and nodded and thanked his hosts. He seemed like any other weary traveler who got sleepier as his belly grew full. But all the while he was secretly on the alert. He overheard the Deer people talking, and out of the corner of his eye he watched everything Poug'tjin'-skwes said and did. Whenever she thought Glous'gap was not looking at her, the lovely *sagama*'s eyes narrowed in contempt, and she licked her lips and smiled.

As he lolled by the fire, Glous'gap noticed especially that the witch held many hastily whispered conversations with the young women of the band, and he also noticed that the young men seemed especially timid. Any time one of them started to say something, that man's wife or Poug'tjin'skwes herself would freeze him into silence with one glance. Moreover, he noticed that all the elders, men and women alike, remained silent, yet kept looking over at him with pleading eyes, as though there were something too frightening to speak of out loud.

From what he saw and heard, Glous'gap could guess what had been going on. After losing the fight over the boy in the birchbark box, Poug'tjin'skwes must have made her way to the home of these Deer people, where she wormed her way into power until she declared herself *sagama* over them. Then she began teaching the young women of the tribe all her evil ways, her wicked incantations, and chants. Ever since her last defeat at Glous'gap's hands, she was determined to prove to herself and her followers how she was the stronger being. Day and night, she dreamed of nothing but killing Glous'gap and taking his place. No one knows why for certain, but some say that once in the dawn of time Poug'tjin'skwes greatly admired the handsome young M'toulin, only to find that he ignored her again and again, since he had no wish to be friendly with those who wielded dark powers. Perhaps his refusal to pay any attention to her had spawned her towering hatred.

Glous'gap passed several days at the village of the Deer people. No hunting party was planned to set out soon. He still wanted to see the Deer people's special dance, but by now he was even more intrigued to discover what mischief Poug'tjin'skwes might be plotting. As for her, Poug'tjin'-skwes hung about Glous'gap and flirted with him as she might with any single young traveler. She was sure he had no idea of her true identity.

One early morning she came by Glous'gap's wigwam where he sat outside, enjoying the sunrise. Poug'tjin'skwes lowered her eyes, as though she were a bashful young woman. She asked him, "Oh, Glous'gap, could you please take me out to sea with you in your canoe, your beautiful white *kwi'den*? I've never seen the islands just off our shores, and I should so love to know them!"

Glous'gap could tell she was up to some trick, but he agreed, and they set forth out across the summer sea.

Poug'tjin'skwes did not offer to help paddle, as any ordinary woman of our people would. Instead she lay back in the stern of the canoe and trailed her hand languidly in the salt water of the bay. In a soft voice she asked Glous'-gap many questions that were designed to draw him into her spell and sap his power. But Glous'gap just paddled forward with mighty strokes and grunted in reply. He thought to himself, *"A'io,* she seeks only to do me great harm!"

When they were far out to sea she called forward to him, "Oh, dear Glous'gap, I'm so very hungry! Let's find a place to gather some gulls' eggs. Then we can eat and perhaps rest together in the shade of a rock!"

Glous'gap nodded and headed toward a barren islet in

the middle of the bay. When they beached, she smiled sweetly and said, "Why don't I wait here with the canoe while you go search out the eggs, and then we'll have a delicious meal together?"

Glous'gap made his way around the point to a wind-blown, spray-drenched place where gulls loved to gather. The rocks were splashed white with the seabirds' droppings, and their many nests were tucked into crannies safely above the tideline. Just at that moment all the Gull people were off fishing for a tasty school of herring, and Glous'gap quickly gathered up a half-dozen or so of their speckled eggs before those *ma'gwis'ag* could return.

As soon as Glous'gap was out of sight, Poug'tjin'skwes cackled to herself, shoved the canoe off into the waters of the bay, and paddled away with all her sorceress's strength, as pleased with herself as she could be. With all her pride, even she could scarcely believe she had bested Glous'gap so easily! "Let's see how long the Lord of Men and Beasts lasts with nothing but gulls' eggs to eat and salt water to drink!" she thought to herself. She laughed as she pictured Glous'gap's carcass dried out on that desolate place. As the little outcropping of black rocks receded in the distance, she looked over her shoulder and began to sing a victory song. This is the song she sang:

> *I've stranded Glous'gap on that island!*
> *I'll take his place amongst Creation!*
> *By my hand he was done in,*
> *I've stolen him from friends and kin!*

I've stranded Glous'gap on that island!
I shall be chief of all Creation!
All the world sings of my power
Poug'tjin'skwes ag' bou'win wa'dagan!

Shouting her arrogant song into the breeze and sea swell, Poug'tjin'skwes set her course straight for the village of the Deer people, the village she had claimed for her own, certain that Glous'gap was vanquished once and for all.

When Glous'gap returned from egg-hunting to the spot where he'd left Poug'tjin'skwes, he found the witch gone. He could just make out the tiny white speck that was his stolen canoe, and he could hear her boastful song drifting faintly back to him on the offshore wind. But as usual Glous'gap was not in any hurry to act, and no worry creased his brow. He sat down calmly on a comfortable rock and gazed across the waters of the beautiful summer bay. He cracked open one egg, and then another and another. He sucked out the delicious insides, savored them in his mouth for a while, and then swallowed the yolks and whites in satisfying gulps. Glous'gap enjoyed his lunch very much, sitting there on his rock in the summer sun and salt air. "Too bad my sister left before we could have our little feast!" he said to himself as he wiped his lips and chuckled.

At last he stood up and stretched. "So that witch thinks she's done me in, eh?" he said aloud to the rocks and the waves washing ashore. "Well, we'll just see who is more powerful!" Then he reached into the mooseskin bag tied to his belt and brought forth his *goun'dow'sen,* his stone-bowled pipe, and some *toum'a'we,* the tobacco he always carried with him. Now ever since Glous'gap obtained the pipe from the blood-stained eagle-cliffs far to the southwest, smoking the *goun'dow'sen* has been a way for Micmac people to pray to the Creator and concentrate our thoughts. As the thin blue-gray smoke wafted around him, Glous'gap considered the best way of dealing with Poug'tjin'skwes.

Finally deciding upon his course, Glous'gap laid aside his pipe and began to sing. The tide was coming in now, and the wind was up a little. Amid the noise of the surf, his voice rose and echoed around the rookery until it was answered by those very *ma'gwis'ag* whose eggs he had been gathering.

"Who calls us?" cried the gulls, as in one voice. "Eh? Who are you, who are you, you? Speak, speak speak, oh, you!"

Glous'gap, who understands the language of all peoples and creatures, called out to the gulls, "My relatives, I need to get back to the mainland! The witch Poug'tjin'skwes has stolen my canoe and believes she has marooned me here on your island to die of thirst. I call upon you and ask with all respect for your help."

"What would you have us do, do, do, eh, you? the gulls called down, circling and swooping as their wings gleamed in the slanting afternoon sun. "You're much too heavy for us to carry, you, you, you!"

"Eh, that's true!" Glous'gap replied. Then he shrunk himself to seven inches tall, and asked, "Am I easier to carry now? Tell me, do, do, do!"

One of the largest gulls dropped down from the sky and landed right beside Glous'gap. He looked at the great M'toulin first with one eye, and then cocked his head to peer at him with the other. After a moment the gull spoke, saying, "Eh, wonderful! It's true, true, true!"

Glous'gap just beamed at the gull. "*A'io*, brother *Magwis*," he said as he climbed on the gull's upper back. "Shall we go now?" He clasped his legs around the bird's neck and hung on tight to the thick feathers of his ruff. Behind Glous'gap, the gull's wings could beat strong and free. The gull started running and hopped once, twice, on his big yellow feet, all the while flapping his great gray, black-tipped wings. Even with the weight of his passenger, the bird lifted easily from the ground. Soon he and Glous'gap were soaring aloft, surveying all the bay below them. From his perch Glous'gap could see the mainland in the distance. It looked like the flat thin line of a hunting cord at first but soon took on the shape of familiar coves, headlands, and low hills.

Glous'gap clung fast to the gull as they glided upon the wind. They were still quite a ways from the shore when Glous'gap sighted Poug'tjin'skwes in his canoe. He leaned forward and said to the gull, "My brother, there is my *kwi'den* and the witch who stole it! Bring me closer so that I can leap from your back into the canoe."

As they swooped closer, Glous'gap hollered down,

"Poug'tjin'skwes, you witch! I am coming now to take back what is mine!"

At the sound of Glous'gap's voice, Poug'tjin'skwes stopped in mid-stroke, gripping the paddle tightly. She craned her neck and looked all around, but she saw nothing save a lone gull riding the air currents. She watched as it circled several times above her, then gasped when she made out the tiny figure of Glous'gap peering down at her from the gull's gleaming back.

"*Uk'se!* Horrors!" she screamed. "Here comes my enemy! Indeed, now I behold the one I thought dead!"

The sight panicked and maddened her, and like a starving wolf chasing a rabbit she lost control of herself and let anger control her instead. In desperation Poug'-tjin'skwes began to summon up a great squall. The storm blew up and howled over huge waves. Lightning flashed, and the sky darkened. The wind ripped and salt spray stung Glous'gap's face, but he never once lost his seat on the gull. From the canoe in which she rode the wildly pitching swells, Poug'tjin'skwes heard his voice coming down to her from above. "I know you and your ways, you evil one!" he called out.

Then Glous'gap leaped lightly from the gull's back into the canoe, regaining his full height as soon as his feet touched down. Angered that so mean a creature dared to misuse the power of nature against him, he ripped the paddle from the witch's grasp and said sternly, "A warrior knows when to talk, when to fight, and when to walk away. I am not impressed by your feeble tricks." Then he dipped his paddle in the water, heading the canoe toward shore. By now the storm Poug'tjin'skwes had conjured up had subsided, and the witch herself cowered in the stern, wet and shivering. Once they beached Glous'gap leaped ashore and set off toward the village of the Deer people, leaving Poug'tjin'skwes to wallow in her shame.

Poug'tjin'skwes, once more humiliated by Glous'gap, fled from the presence of human beings and ran through the woods shrieking like a crazed animal, her heart filled with bitterness, spite, and malice. There no doubt after a while she recovered her pride and began biding her time, waiting for another chance to confront the mighty Glous'gap.

Our stories do not tell us whether Glous'gap was able to make things right with the Deer people while they served under the witch's reign, or whether he finally got to see the Deer Dance after all. But we know for sure he was not yet done with Poug'tjin'skwes, and he always remained grateful to the *mag'wis'ag*, the Gull people.

GLOUS'GAP AND WA'SIS

Wodin'it atog'agan Glous'gapi...

GLOUS'GAP, the great spirit warrior and champion of all Wabanaki peoples, had a busy time of it in the old days, when he was putting things to right. He conquered a whole race of evil giants, as well as the Mitoug'oul'in, the wicked sorcerers. He rid the world of Pa'mola, a wicked spirit who walks by night, and many other ogres, cannibals, and witches as well. One day he boasted to a woman, "There is nothing left for me to do, for I have conquered all the beings around here who needed conquering!"

The woman only laughed, and asked, "Do you truly think so, Glous'gap? I know of one who has never been conquered, and no one can get the best of him."

Glous'gap raised his eyebrows in surprise. "What is the name of this being?" he demanded. "Bring me before his wigwam!"

"He is called Wa'sis," the woman said, "and I think you should stay clear of him, for there is no winning any battle with this one." Nevertheless, she led the way to her own lodge, and Glous'gap lifted the doorflap, ready to confront this formidable being called Wa'sis.

Glous'gap was surprised to see that Wa'sis was nothing but a baby, a chubby fellow with a shock of black hair and eyes as brown as berries. He sat on the dirt floor of the wigwam, singing a little song to himself and sucking on a piece of maple sugar. Glous'gap smiled at the baby, and the baby smiled back at him.

Glous'gap had no wife, and he knew nothing about caring for babies. Still, he was sure he could get this little one to obey him. "Come here," he commanded Wa'sis.

But Wa'sis didn't move. He just sat there sucking on that maple sugar, staring at Glous'gap.

Glous'gap was angry that this being would not do his bidding. He was the Lord of Men and Beasts, after all, and he was not accustomed to such treatment. He hollered in a terrible threatening tone, "I TOLD YOU TO COME HERE RIGHT NOW!"

At that Wa'sis set up a squall, completely drowning out Glous'gap's voice. The baby's tiny face twisted awry in utter despair, and he stuck out his quivering lower lip as he turned an ugly shade of red. Huge tears splashed down on his round little belly, and the noise of his crying was unbearable.

Glous'gap tried every trick he knew to amuse Wa'sis. He imitated the song of the bluebird. He tickled Wa'sis under the chin with some bluejay feathers. Still, Wa'sis would not stop crying until he was good and ready. Thoroughly confounded, Glous'gap now drew upon all his magical powers to try to impress Wa'sis. He recited spells and incantations. He even sang the songs that raise the dead, and those that send Matjou'andou, the Evil One, scurrying down to the places we never hear of, but Wa'sis ignored it all. He just sat there sucking on his maple sugar, looking bored.

Finally Glous'gap gave in. He ran out of the wigwam, past the child's amused mother, while Wa'sis remained sitting on the floor, calling, "Goo! Goo!"

And to this day, our people say that whenever a baby says "Goo!" he is remembering the time when Wa'sis triumphed over Glous'gap.

GLOUS'GAP AND THE
THREE WISHES

Wodin'it atog'agan Glous'gapi . . .

GLOUS'GAP, Lord of Beasts and Human Beings, began to tell the people, "Before too long I am going to leave you. I'm going on ahead to prepare a place for all of you. But between now and the time I go, I will grant the wishes of anybody who cares to come and ask me for something."

Three *oulno'ag*, or Indian men, one older and two younger, decided to seek out the M'toulin, and as always for those who would find Glous'gap, they had a hard seven years of it. When they were still three months' journey away from the lodge, they heard the honking outcry sent up by Glous'gap's watch-geese, and they rejoiced because the noise told them they must be getting close. At last they located the lodge on a little pine island in the middle of a lake. Then Glous'gap hushed his geese and welcomed the visitors. He entertained them with feasting and songs and finally asked them, "What does each of you want most as a gift from me?"

The eldest was a plain man who was not well-respected in his home village because he had no skill or luck when it came to hunting. He told Glous'gap, "I should like to become good at catching and killing game so I can better provide for my family."

Glous'gap nodded and gave the man a flute. The sweet notes that came from it enticed all game animals toward the flute player. The man turned the flute over wonderingly in his hands. Then he looked up and thanked Glous'gap and set off happily toward his home.

When Glous'gap asked the second man what wish he would like to have granted, he grinned wolfishly, and said, "I want the love of many women!"

"How many?" Glous'gap asked.

The man laughed, "I don't care exactly how many

women there are, just as long as there are enough, and more than enough!"

Glous'gap frowned at this response, but nonetheless he handed over to the man a large leather bag wonderfully decorated with dyed porcupine quills. It was tightly tied at the neck, and Glous'gap cautioned him, "Do not open this bag until you reach your lodge, no matter what." So that young man thanked Glous'gap, and he too began to make his way home.

The third man was handsome, carefree, and altogether a foolish young fellow. All he cared about was making people laugh. When Glous'gap asked him what gift he wanted most of all, he giggled and said, "I'd like to be able to burp and break wind any time I want to!"

You see, in the olden times among the Wabanaki peoples, such sounds were always greeted by the people with laughter, and this man thought an endless supply of farts and belches would make him very popular. Glous'gap raised his eyebrows, but he said nothing. Instead, he went a little way off into the woods and plucked a certain root which once eaten was sure to make the young man's belly quickly swell with gas.

"Don't eat this root until you get back to your village!" Glous'gap warned as he handed it over. The giddy young man thanked Glous'gap as he tucked the root in his little buckskin pouch and set out for home.

As with all who seek out Glous'gap, the return journey of all three of these men should have taken only seven days. But of these three, only one man returned quickly and happily to his lodge. That was the man who wished to become a good hunter. He headed home with his flute in his hand and peace in his heart, smiling because he knew that as long as he lived, he would always have enough meat to feed his family.

As for the other two, one never reached home at all, and the other was so miserable it didn't much matter whether he reached his home or not, as you shall hear.

Now the young man who yearned for the love of women was afire with curiosity to open the bag Glous'gap had given him, and he hadn't gotten very far from Glous'gap's lodge before he untied the deerskin thong. Out of that bag came flying white doves by the hundreds. The gleaming flock wheeled and dipped about him, and suddenly all those doves were transformed into beautiful young women with eyes like glowing coals and swirling black hair. Uttering passionate little cooing cries, they crowded around him, throwing their arms about him and hungrily kissing him. At first he was delighted, but as they mobbed him in even greater numbers he began to be afraid. "Give me space to catch my breath!" he cried out, but they would not. When he tried to escape, the throng of dove-women forced him to the ground by their sheer weight and pinned him there, squirming beneath them. And in that way, squashed flat and begging for breath, he smothered to death beneath the churning, cooing mass of dove-women. Later that day, people passing along the trail found his tattered remains. The dove-women had vanished, and to this day no one knows where they went.

The third man, the carefree young fool, started out merrily along the path back to his village. He always paid so little attention to what was going on around him that he didn't even remember that Glous'gap had given him any gift at all until he was halfway home. Suddenly he stopped in his tracks and struck himself on the forehead. "Ooh!" he exclaimed, "I almost forgot! That nice Glous'gap gave me this great windy present! I wonder if eating that root will really work?" He forgot all about Glous'gap's warning in his eagerness to begin making rude sounds, and he snatched the root from his pouch and bolted it down. Scarcely had he swallowed it when his belly swelled hugely with gas, and he realized with delight that he had the power to belch and fart to his heart's content. The noises he made echoed across the land, alarming the animals and resounding from the hills. The young man said to himself, "Oh, this is truly wonderful!" and he went on his way, trumpeting before and behind him, happy as a meadowlark.

Before too long, the foolish young man began to grow tired his own endless stream of burps and farts. By now he was hungry and in need of rest. Spotting a deer in a clearing just ahead, he nocked an arrow to his bow and stole even closer. He was just about to let fly the arrow when in spite of himself he loudly farted. The deer bounded away, and the young man could only stretch out his arms and cried out "Come back!" as he watched it disappear among the trees.

That foolish man who had wished so much to fart and belch soon realized that his gift made all hunting impossible. As it was already late in the fall, there was little food to sustain him on his journey home. By the time he reached his village, he was half-dead from hunger. "But now," he told himself, "I'll be able to use this gift to make myself popular with everybody!"

At first, the people did laugh every time he burped or farted. But very soon the villagers got bored with his endless smelly noises and began to avoid him. At last he felt that his life was not worth living, and he crept off into the woods to die alone.

So you see, there are good reasons to think carefully about what we wish or pray for. We may well get exactly what we asked for—and more in the bargain.

GLOUS'GAP'S
FAREWELL

Wodin'it atog'agan Glous'gapi . . .

THE DAY FINALLY CAME that Glous'gap had often spoken of, the day when he was to depart for the North and leave us. He readied his white canoe, the one that sometimes looks like an ordinary canoe and sometimes takes the form of a whole island. Once he had gathered up his maplewood bow and his magic arrows, he was set to leave. But there were certain things the Lord of Beasts and Human Beings needed to tell our people before he went away. On a beach of the Sunrise Ocean he called together the people and the birds and animals to hear what he had to say. The crowd was hushed and sad. Everyone was trying to imagine what life without Glous'gap would be like.

One elder stood and addressed Glous'gap. "Our ancestors were hopelessly lost when you first came to walk among us many snows ago," he said. "Our people were on a journey from a distant land across the Great Waters of the East, but they moved in darkness. They did not even know what they were looking for. It was you who led us to this northland of lakes and forests, where the sea teems with fish and deer walk quietly in the woods, this land you yourself helped the Creator to prepare for us. You taught us how to make canoes and lodges and how to hunt and fish. It was you who taught our medicine-people how to heal. It was you who taught us how to behave toward one another and how to govern ourselves. For all these things, we thank you. But how shall we live without you?"

Glous'gap chose his words carefully. "By now, I have taught you all you need to know in order to live well in this world," he replied. "You may fear that this is not the case, but it is so. And when the time comes, I promise you I will return. Only one thing remains to be given to you, and that is a knowledge of things that will come to pass before I come back to walk among you once more. I'm going to give you that knowledge now."

Glous'gap spoke slowly, and the people listened very hard. They knew they must remember every word Glous'gap was saying to them.

"I see warriors of the Serpent peoples moving northward from their southern villages," Glous'gap began. "They are led by one called the Black Turtle. Your own bands will move northward and have an uneasy alliance with them for a time, but a great war will break out among their own confederacy, bringing that peace to an end. War, death, and pillage come with the Serpents."

"Another invasion then will come down from the north, along the land of the sunset far to the west of here. Those who come are the Brush-wolf peoples. With them they bring chaos, and the far-scattered bands of your people who encounter them will take to the forest, banding together in senseless warfare. Remember this and tell your children."

Glous'gap closed his eyes, and it was clear that he was seeing in his inner sight all the dire things he was predicting. "Far off is another invasion," Glous'gap continued. "In enormous canoes bearded men are coming from across the Great Waters of the Sunrise. Those wooden canoes are as many as the snowflakes of winter. These people are white, and they are like hungry, unenlightened children. They will take this land and its lakes and forests away from you. They will almost destroy it, but the time of the destroyers will come to an end. When their children become as your children, then their time closes."

The crowd stirred uneasily, thinking about the terrible

things Glous'gap foretold. They did not wish to be invaded and dispossessed, but if Glous'gap said it was going to happen, they knew it was true. Somewhere in the crowd a child started to cry, but its mother hushed it. All wanted to hear what Glous'gap would say next.

Now the Lord of Beasts and Human Beings opened his eyes and smiled at the people. His love for them shone in his eyes. "I am going far to the north to make a place for you," he told them. "No person can come there while still alive. You can travel there only after you die in this earthly world. I say to you, build your wigwams facing the sunrise, and wait for my return. Always live your lives in a sacred manner, just as I have been teaching you to do all along. If you fail to do so, remember that there is a place of Darkness that lasts forever, and that is where you will come to dwell."

"Do not worry," he ended by telling them. "I will come back to you. I will raise you up from the burial mounds, and I will call you down from the scaffolds of the tree burials. I'll return. Watch for me!"

Now it was truly time to say goodbye, and Glous'gap passed among the crowd of people and creatures, with a word for each one. He patted his old friend Fisher on his sleek head, and waved at Gopher who had helped him subdue the giant moose. Hardest of all for Glous'gap to take leave of were his dogs and his dearest friends and relatives, kindly Mrs. Bear, brave Pine Martin, and good-natured Grandfather Turtle. They wept at the thought of parting with him, but they knew that Glous'gap was doing what he had to do and going where he had to go.

Glous'gap seated himself in his canoe that gleamed white as a glacier. As he began paddling north along the shoreline, his watch-geese set up a loud honking salute of farewell. After he paddled a little farther out, Bootup the Whale joined him and swam along beside him for a bit to keep him company. Then she fell back, spouting goodbye, and soon Glous'gap's canoe looked to those on shore like only the tiniest speck on the horizon. At last even that speck disappeared, and Glous'gap was gone.

Today, our people still think back on Glous'gap's last words to us. We know of things that have come to pass, just as he foretold. Sure enough, Iroquoian people came up from the south and invaded our territories, and we had many years of grievous warfare with them. Sure enough, the Navajos and the Apaches came down from Alaska into the southwestern part of the land, where the Little Summer Woman dwells. And just as Glous'gap said, the white people came. Now much of our land is lost to us, and that same land has suffered greatly under the white people's keeping of it.

Is the time yet upon us that Glous'gap spoke of, the time when the white people's children shall become as our children, and their rule will be ended, and Glous'gap will come back to walk among us? No one is certain. We can only try to live as he taught us. Always, we wait for his return.

LAND OF THE MICMAC

Land of the Micmac and their allies where Glous'gap tracked Win'pe the Sorcerer.

Mak'toog'wek (Saint Lawrence River)

Gaspege'o'akik (Gaspé Peninsula)

Passa'moog'waddy (Pleasant Point, Maine)

E'peg'wit'akik (Prince Edward Island)

Pictou (Pictou, Nova Scotia)

Ouna'mag'ik (Cape Breton Island)

Uk'tuk'kam'kou (Newfoundland)

Uk'tji'gum (Atlantic Ocean)

MICMAC GLOSSARY AND PRONUNCIATION GUIDE

A

Abenaki (ah-behn-AH kee) / ***Abanaki*** (A-bahn-AH-kee): People of the Sunrise.

Abenakik (ah-behn-AH-keek): Land of the Abenaki Indians.

abi'stan'outj (ah-bee-stahn-OOCH): pine marten.

abi'tes (ah-BEE-tehz): girl.

a'bo'goun'um'we (ah-boh-goon-um-WEH): help, help me.

a'dou'dou'gwetj (ah-doo-doo-GWEHJ): squirrel.

agam'oug (ah-gam-OOK): snowshoes.

a'io (ah-YOH): yes, affirmative.

a'tigan'igan (ah-tee-gahn-EE-gahn): cradleboard.

a'tog'agan (ah-took-AH-gahn): a story.

a'tog'agan'it (ah-took-ah-gahn-ID): It is a story.

B

ba'bitj (bah-BEEJ): a leather thong.

bag'a'tou'we (bahg-ah-doo-WEH): lacrosse or field hockey.

basp (BAHSP): crush it.

bootup (BOO-tahp): whale.

bootup'skwes (boo-TAHP-skwehz): she-whale.

bou'win'wa'dagan (boo-ween-wah -DAHG-ahn): witch-craft or sorcery.

C

Chic-chouc (SHICK-shook): mountains on the Gaspé Peninsula.

G

gaspe (GAHZ-peh): land's end (from *gous'pe*, KOOZ-peh).

gitji (GHEE-jee): great.

gitji'ke'napi (GHEE-jee-keh-NAHB-ee): great man of power; great warrior.

Gitji Manitou (GHEE-jee mahn-ee-TOO): the Great Spirit; God.

Glous'gap (glooz-KAHB): Wabanaki cultural hero.

Glous'gapi (glooz-KAH-bee): same as above.

goun'dow'sen (goon-DOW-sen): the sacred stone-bowl pipe.

K

k'tin (kah-DEEN): Do you have . . . ?

K'tin tumakun ak tum'a'we? (kah-DEEN toom-AH-gahn AHG toom-ah-WEH): Do you have a pipe and tobacco?

kamsok (KAHMZ-ook): High bluffs.

Kes'poog'wit (kehz- POOGH-weet): Yarmouth, Nova Scotia.

Kesik (GEH-seek): winter personified.

Kesoulk (Keh-SOOLK): the Creator; God.

ko'gan (KOH-gahn): fish scum found on water.

ko'ko'kas (koh-KOH-kahz): owl.

kous (KOOZ): stop. Also written as *Gahs*.

koussal (koos-SAHL): hurry.

kwa'bit (kwah-BEED): beaver.

kwa'bit'tjitj (kwah-beed-TJITJ): little beaver.

kwi'den (KWEE-dehn): canoe.

M

m'te'oulin (meh-teh-OO-lehn): true medicine; the ancient knowledge path.

M'toulin (meh-DOO-lehn): practitioner of *m'te'oulin*.

Mala'sit'akik (mah-lah-seet-AH-keek): land of the Malaseet Indians.

Mak'toog'wek (mahk'-TOOG-'wehk): original name of the Saint Lawrence River.

mag'gak (MAHG-gahk): a type of birchbark basket.

ma'gwis (MAH-gweez): seagull.

ma'gwis'ag (mah-KWEEZ-ahk): seagulls.

manitou (mahn-ee-TOO): spirit.

Matjou'andou (mah-JOO ahn-DOO): the Evil One; the devil.

matta'es (maht-tah-EHS): porcupine.

Me'toug'ou'lin (meh-toog-OO-lehn): a race of giant sorcerers.

Micmac (MICK-mack) : English rendering of *Migoum'ag* (Mee-GOOM-ahk), which has three basic meanings—"relatives," "allies," and "The Turtle People."

Migoum'agi (mee-goom-AH-kee): land of the Micmac Indians.

Mi'goum'wes'oug (mee-goom-WEHZ-ook): helping spirits; a race of little people.

mik'tjitj (meek -JEEJ): turtle.

mo'kwe (moh-KWEH): emphatic no.

Moon'as'tabagan'kwi'tje'an'nook? (moon-ahz-tah-BAHgahn kwee-jeh AHN nook): Isn't the land showing itself plain as a bowstring?

Moonanook (moon-ah-NOOK): Grand Manan Island.

Mouin-agou (moo-een-AH-goo): Mrs. Bear.

mous'i'gisk (mooz-ee-GEESK): spirits of the air.

N

nigsgam (NEEG-sgahm): Holy Grandfather, another name for God.

nigsgam'itj (neeg-sgahm-EEJ): grandfather.

nou'goum'i (noo-goom-EE): my grandmother; my granny; my relative.

nou'goum'itj (noo-goom-EEJ): grandmother.

nou'tjitj (noo-JEEJ): grandchild.

O

O'gum'ke'ge'ok (oh-goom-keh-GEH-ohk): Liverpool, Nova Scotia.

O'gum'ke'ok (oh-goom-KEH-ohk): Moser River, Nova Scotia.

oul'nap'skouk (ool-NAHP-skook): wampum shell.

Oul'no'ag (ool-NOH-ahg): human beings; term used for the Micmac people.

Oun'a'mag'ik (oon-ah-MAHG-eek): Cape Breton Island.

P

Pa'mola (bah-MOH-lah): wicked spirit of the night; also a word for the nighthawk.

Passa'moog'waddy (pah-za-mook-wah-DEE): Passama-quoddy Indian township of Pleasant Point, near Eastport, Maine.

pe'gumk (PEH-goomk): the fisher, a member of the weasel family.

Penobscot'akik (pehn-ohb-skaht-AH-keek): land belonging to the Penobscot Indians of the state of Maine.

Pictou (PEEK-tou): the place of the bubbling waters.

Poug'tjin'skwes (poog-ZJEHN-skwehz): name of a witch who troubled Glous'gap.

S

sagama (sah-GAHM-ah): chief.

'skwes (SKWEHZ): female; woman.

T

tami'a'lin (tah-mee-ah-LEEN): Where are you going?

tas'goum (TAHZ-goom): snake, serpent.

te'am (TEH-am): moose.

te'am'mous'e (teh-ahm-MOUZ-eh): He strips things off trees.

tja'pi (ZJAH-bee): come.

tji'nou (JEE-noo): cannibal.

tji'pitj'gam (jee-PEEJ-gahm): giant wingless horned serpent.

tou'lada'doul'dim'kewe (too-lah-dah-DOOL-deem KEH-weh): Micmac phrase of greeting.

toum'a'we (toom-AH-weh): tobacco.

toum'we (TOOM-weh): tobacco.

u

uk'se (OOK-seh): oh, horror!

Uk'tuk'kam'kou (ook-took-KAHM-koo): Newfoundland.

Uk'tu'tun (ook-TOO-toon): Cape North, Cape Breton Island.

Uk'tji'boog'took (ook-jee-BOOG-took): Halifax, Nova Scotia.

Uk'tjig'oum (ook-JEEG oom): ocean.

up'kous'un (oob-KOOZ-ahn): necklace.

up'sakum'ote (oob-sah-kahm-OH-teh): medicine bag or pouch.

Utj'bak'tasum (OOJ-bahk-tahz-ahm): Young Wolf, Glous'gap's brother.

utj'kin (OOJ-keen): younger brother.

W

wa'wan (WAH-wan): egg.

Wabanaki (wah'bahn-AH-kee): People of the Dawn or Sunrise. 1. The Passamaquoddy Indians. 2. The combined tribes and bands of the Wabanaki Alliance, including the Micmac, Malaseet, Passamaquoddy, Penobscot, and Abenaki peoples.

Wabanakik (wah-bahn-AH-keek): land of the Passamaquoddy; land of the Dawn people.

wa'gook (WAH-gook): vermin.

wa'sis (WAH-seez): baby.

was'ouk (WAHZ-ook): sky; Sky World.

wast'ow (WAHZT-ow): snow.

Win'pe (WEEN-peh): an evil sorcerer who fought Glous'gap.

wis'koug'wow (weez-KOOG-wow): cooking pot.

witj'kwid lakun'tjitj (WEEJ-kweed lahk-ahn-JEEJ): small birchbark dish.

Wodin'it atog'agan (woh-DEHN-eet ah-toog-AH-gahn): This is a story . . .

woltes'takun (wohl-tehs-TAHK-ahn): wooden bowl.

Wotju'san (woh-JOO-sahn): the monster Wind Bird.

FURTHER READING
AND VIEWING

Books

Bruchac, Joseph, *Return of the Sun: Native American Tales From The Northeast Woodlands* (Crossing Press, 1990). An excellent collection of Native American stories by this Abenaki author, scholar, and storyteller.

Bruchac, Joseph, *Roots of Survival: Native American Storytelling and the Sacred* (Fulcrum, 1996). A valuable essay collection exploring the nature and uses of native storytelling.

DeBlois, Albert D., *Micmac Texts* (Canadian Museum of Civilization, 1990). A bilingual text aimed mostly at scholars.

Leland, Charles G. *Algonquin Legends* (Houghton Mifflin, 1894; reprinted by Dover Publications, 1992), illustrated with copies of old drawings on birchbark. Although the anthropological interpretations and the diction are dated, this book is still of interest.

Rand, Silas, *Legends of the Micmac* (Longmans, Green, & Co., 1894). The Reverend Rand, a missionary in Nova Scotia, compiled the first Micmac dictionary. Like Leland's (above), this book is dated but still of interest.

Whitehead, Ruth Holmes, *Micmac: How Their Ancestors Lived Five Hundred Years Ago* (Nimbus Publishing, 1983).

Whitehead, Ruth Holmes, *The Old Man Told Us: Excerpts from Micmac History 1500-1950* (Nimbus Publishing, 1991). An excellent introduction to Micmac history and culture. Whitehead, an ethnologist at the Nova Scotia Museum, intersperses a running narrative of Micmac history with a wealth of documents and oral histories. There are also a number of photographs.

Whitehead, Ruth Holmes, *Stories from The Six Worlds: Micmac Legends* (Nimbus Publishing, 1989).

Whitehead, Ruth Holmes, *Six Micmac Stories* (Nimbus Publishing, 1989), illustrated with old-style Micmac drawings.

Film

Alanis Obomsawin's CBC documentary film, "Incident at Restigouche," gives a powerful account of the Micmac's struggle over fishing rights and tribal sovereignty in Quebec in the summer of 1981.

ABOUT THE AUTHORS

MICHAEL B. RUNNINGWOLF, a Micmac Algonquin, was born in 1953 and grew up on both sides of the Maine/ Canadian border, in Searsport and Freeport, Maine, and in Big Cove (Rexton area), New Brunswick. He is a direct descendant of Beminuit, the Grand Chief of the Micmac Nation, as well as of the Clement and Noel bloodlines. Since the seventeenth century, his relatives and family have been the primary source for much information supplied to anthropologists about Micmac culture and tradition.

Formerly an instructor at the University of New Mexico and an interpretive park ranger for the New Mexico State Parks Division, Michael B. RunningWolf currently makes his living as a Native storyteller and crafts- man. He lives in Los Lunas, New Mexico.

PATRICIA CLARK SMITH was born in 1943 in Holyoke, Massachusetts, and is of Irish, French-Canadian, and Micmac descent. She grew up in Northampton, Massachusetts, and in Portland, Maine. She was educated at Smith College and at Yale University, where she earned a Ph.D. in English. She has been awarded many grants and honors, including a Woodrow Wilson Fellowship, the Las Campañas teaching award, a Rockefeller Research Grant, and a Fulbright Faculty Development Grant. Among her published works are *As Long as the Rivers Flow: The Stories of Nine Native Americans* (with Paula Gunn Allen), *Changing Your Story: Poems, and Western Literature in a World Context* (co-editor).

Patricia Clark Smith teaches Native American literature and creative writing at the University of New Mexico, Albuquerque.